UTAH

IRON HORSE LEGACY
BOOK NINE

ELLE JAMES

TWISTED PAGE INC

UTAH

IRON HORSE LEGACY BOOK #9

New York Times & USA Today
Bestselling Author

ELLE JAMES

Copyright © 2023 by Elle James

All rights reserved.

No part of this book may be reproduced in any form or by any electronic or mechanical means, including information storage and retrieval systems, without written permission from the author, except for the use of brief quotations in a book review.

© 2023 Twisted Page Inc. All rights reserved.

EBOOK ISBN: 978-1-62695-508-0

ISBN PRINT: 978-1-62695-509-7

Dedicated to my family who puts up with my crazy deadlines and keeps things running when I'm writing. Love you all so very much!
Elle James

AUTHOR'S NOTE

Enjoy other books in this series by Elle James

Iron Horse Legacy
Soldier's Duty (#1)
Ranger's Baby (#2)
Marine's Promise (#3)
SEAL's Vow (#4)
Warrior's Resolve (#5)
Drake (#6)
Grimm (#7)
Murdock (#8)
Utah (#9)
Judge (#10)

Visit ellejames.com for more titles and release dates
Join her newsletter at
https://ellejames.com/contact/

CHAPTER 1

"Again, Fly!" Spike shouted. "PJ here, says you're the best knife thrower of all the recruits. So far, I'm not impressed." The tattooed man with the slick, bald head and a wife-beater tank top stood beside her, his meaty arms folded over his chest.

She hated being called Fly, but it was better than some of the names a few recruits were called. No one went by their given names. They weren't even allowed to share their real names with other recruits.

Liza glanced over at the woman standing ten feet from her, throwing knives at her own target. She went by PJ. The woman didn't glance in their direction when her name was mentioned. Instead, she kept throwing the knives, her face blank, free of any emotion. Always the best course of action at The Camp. Mind your own business and never show your feelings. They'd use them against you.

Exhausted after a full day's strenuous training, Liza Gray's aim was off. She was tired, her muscles ached, and she didn't feel like throwing.

Not that she had a choice. Refusing orders wasn't tolerated. The response was usually harsh and painful. She'd had enough pain the past ten months to last a lifetime.

Liza plucked one of the eight-inch, stainless steel throwing knives from the nylon sheath strapped to her leg. Holding the flat sides between her thumb and forefinger, she focused on the paper silhouette target attached to a stack of hay bales, cocked her arm and sent the knife cutting through the air with deadly accuracy, striking the paper victim in the heart.

On more than one occasion, she imagined sending a knife straight through Spike's heart—that cold, dead organ in his chest that allowed him to treat the "recruits" like pond scum.

"Mommy," a high-pitched voice sounded behind her.

Liza turned to smile at the golden-haired angel skipping toward her, holding a bright yellow dandelion in her little fist.

"Look what I found." The child held out her hand, her blue eyes bright and happy.

"It's pretty, Tayla." Liza bent to study the flower.

"Did I say we were done here?" The harsh tone yanked her back to reality.

Liza spun to face Spike.

He stalked toward her, his thick eyebrows forming a sharp V over his prominent nose. "I get the feeling you're not giving me your best." He grabbed Tayla's little arm.

"Let go of my daughter." Liza lunged for Spike as he backed away.

"Leave the kid out of it," PJ called out.

"Shut it, PJ," Spike shot back.

PJ shot Spike a narrow-eyed glare and muttered something that sounded suspiciously like *bastard* beneath her breath before launching another knife toward her target.

Spike snorted and returned his attention to Liza. "I don't have to remind you who's in charge, do I?"

"No, sir," Liza said, afraid to make the man angrier. He had a fast and dangerous temper. She eased forward. "Tayla, go to the bunkhouse."

"The brat ain't goin' anywhere." Spike's grip remained firm on the child's arm. "She'll do as I say, and you'll stay where you are, or I'll snap this twig." He tipped his head toward his hand holding her daughter's thin arm.

Liza stood still, her pulse hammering through her veins. She'd seen this man break a teenage boy's arm. It wouldn't take much for him to break Tayla's. Liza didn't dare push the man, or he'd follow through on his threat.

Holding tightly to Tayla's arm, Spike dragged her

to the hay bales and stood her in front of the silhouette target.

Liza's heart lodged in her throat. "What are you doing? Leave her alone. She's just a little girl."

Spike ignored Liza and knelt in front of the three-year-old. "Stay here, or I'll hurt your mommy," he said threateningly.

Tayla leaned to the side and stared at Liza. Her little brows furrowed. "Mommy?"

"It's okay, Tay," Liza tried to reassure her daughter, dread eating a hole in her gut. Nothing was okay. Nothing had been okay for the past ten months since she and Tayla had been brought to The Camp.

Spike pulled the bottom bale out from beneath the stack, lowering the silhouette. Now, the black form rose a foot above Tayla's head. He placed the bale he'd pulled in front of the other bales and lifted Tayla to stand on top, her little body covering much of the black target area. Then he pulled the knife Liza had thrown minutes before from the bale and carried it to her. "Pretend your daughter's life depends on your aim," he said, his tone low and threatening as he held out the knife.

Liza's heart clenched in her chest.

He turned toward Tayla. "Now, hit the target in the head without hitting the girl."

Liza shook her head. "You can't be serious."

He cocked an eyebrow. "If you don't throw the knife, I will."

Liza stared at her daughter.

Tayla stood on the hay bale, a worried crease on her sweet forehead, her bright blond hair pulled back into a braid like all the other girls on the compound.

"Fine," Spike said. "I'll throw." He tossed the knife into the air, caught it between his thumb and forefinger and cocked his arm.

"No!" Liza grabbed his arm before he could throw the blade at Tayla.

"If you don't throw one in ten seconds and hit the silhouette, I will throw the knife." Spike tipped his head back and looked down his nose. "What's it to be?"

"Give me the damned knife," she said between clenched teeth.

"Now, you're listening." He handed her the knife. "Ten."

She took the knife from him and faced Tayla. "Baby, stand very still. Don't move. Not even a little."

Tayla's eyes widened. "I'm scared, Mommy."

"It's okay," Liza said, choking back a sob. "I'm scared, too," she whispered. Then louder, she said, "Close your eyes, Tayla."

"Why?" Tayla's little voice was soft and shaky.

"Nine," Spike continued his countdown.

"Think about all the flowers you can hold in your hands," Liza's words were strangled in her throat. "Close your eyes, baby."

Tayla's eyes fluttered closed.

"Eight."

Liza squeezed her eyes shut for a moment, then opened them again and stared at the only person in her life she gave a damn about.

"Seven…Six…"

She raised the knife.

"Five…Four…"

Breathe in.

Liza pulled in a deep breath and let it out slowly.

"Three…Two…

When all the air left her lungs, she let the knife fly from her fingers.

Her heart stopped, and her world stood still as the stainless-steel blade cleaved the air in what felt like slow motion.

The sharp tip of the dagger struck the black silhouette less than an inch from Tayla's left ear.

Liza sucked in a breath and let it out. Her heart resumed beating, hammering against her ribs and her knees shook. A single tear slipped from the corner of her eye. Thankfully, the eye away from Spike's watchful gaze.

He nodded. "She's ready."

"Good," a deep voice said behind Liza.

She spun to face Commander, the man in charge of everything at The Camp. He intimidated everyone, standing well over six feet tall with a jagged scar running down the right side of his face from the corner of his eyebrow to his jaw. No one knew his real name. From the moment Liza and Tayla had arrived, they'd be forced to call him Commander and respond to him by saying, "Yes, sir."

Spike was the same way. He only went by Spike. No one dared ask what his real name was. If anyone were that stupid, they'd end up punched in the gut or worse.

"Ready for what?" Liza asked and added, "Sir."

Commander stared down his nose at her. "Your first assignment."

Her brow furrowed. "What assignment, sir?"

Spike's lip curled up in a snarl. "We train for a reason, idiot."

The man in charge's eyes narrowed as his gaze swept her from head to toe. "Bring her to the TOC."

Spike popped a salute. "Yes, sir!"

Commander spun on his heels and marched away.

The men and women running The Camp acted as if they'd been in the military or wanted the recruits to think they had. Military precision and discipline were to always be adhered to on the grounds. The only time she could be herself was in the bunkhouse after the guards had left. Only then could Liza hold Tayla, sing to her and tell her stories of happier times and places.

Tayla was one of the youngest children at this location. Liza had heard whispers of other camps.

Several of the newer guards had come from a camp that had been raided and disbanded.

Liza remembered wishing the camp where she and Tayla had been held prisoner would suffer the same demise. If they were raided, they might have a chance to escape.

The guards kept a tight rein on the recruits. Chain-link fencing topped with concertina wire surrounded the compound that had one road leading in and out. The gate was manned by no less than four guards, twenty-four-seven.

In the ten months since Liza had been there, only one recruit had attempted an escape. A seventeen-year-old boy they'd called Teej had managed to dig a hole beneath the fence. In the middle of the night, he'd slipped beneath the wire. Unfortunately, he'd tripped a wire that detonated a claymore mine. Teej died that night. Since then, no one had tried to make a run for freedom.

For the first few weeks, Liza had prayed every night that someone would come to their rescue. No one had. No one cared about the single mother who'd packed everything she and Tayla owned into a beat-up 1977 Chevy pickup and left Valier, Montana, for the big city of Bozeman, hoping to find work to start over and make a life for themselves.

No one would've worried when she hadn't checked in. Liza didn't have anyone left. Her mother had died when she was close to Tayla's age. Her father had passed a year ago, leaving the old truck and just enough money in his bank account to get them to Bozeman.

The father of her child was long gone, having left Valier for Seattle the moment he'd heard Liza was pregnant. He'd denied Tayla was his and refused to help in any way.

No one was coming for them or anyone else in The Camp.

Spike grabbed Liza's arm and shoved her after Commander.

Liza dug in her heels, forcing Spike to a halt. She looked back at the hay bale where Tayla stood. "Go to the bunkhouse, Tayla. I'll see you later."

"Yes, Mommy." Tayla jumped off the bale and ran for the long low building painted the same dull green as the trees surrounding the compound.

Spike let go of Liza's arm. "Stay," he commanded as if to a well-trained dog.

Liza remained where she stood while Spike stepped over to where PJ pulled eight shiny blades out of her target.

His hand clapped down on the woman's shoulder beside her long sandy-blond braid. He leaned close to her ear and whispered something Liza couldn't hear.

PJ turned, a frown denting her forehead, and stared at Liza.

"Do it," Spike said.

PJ's mouth pressed into a thin line. She shoved

her throwing knives into the pouch strapped to her thigh and headed for the bunkhouse.

Spike returned to where Liza stood, planted a hand on her back and sent her stumbling after the disappearing Commander.

She righted herself and marched alongside her trainer, half-running to keep up with his longer strides. He didn't release her arm until they reached the TOC. Liza had learned TOC stood for Tactical Operations Center and always wondered what operations they conducted inside.

She'd never stepped through the doors. The only recruits she'd seen go inside had left The Camp shortly afterward. Only one had returned in all the time she'd been there. He'd been "promoted" to a trainer over the younger recruits as he wasn't much more than a teen himself.

Commander had entered, leaving the door open.

When Liza hesitated, Spike shoved her inside.

She staggered down a hallway with doors on either side and came into a large, open room. Four folding tables were grouped in the middle, with folding chairs lined up on either side. In one corner, an array of six monitors hung from the wall, with images of the camp displayed in real-time.

Liza could see trainers and recruits heading for the mess hall for chow. Her stomach rumbled despite being knotted from apprehension. She'd only had breakfast that day, oatmeal and toast. Lunch usually consisted of beef jerky and water. She'd given her share to one of the other recruits who'd passed out during their morning hand-to-hand combat training.

Spike nudged her. "Show respect."

Tired and scared, Liza sucked in her gut, shoved back her shoulders and stood at attention.

When Commander turned to face her, the scar on his cheek was even more pronounced by the light and shadows cast by the single bulb hanging over his head.

He held out a computer tablet. "This is your assignment."

She took the tablet and stared down at an image of a woman with long black hair, high cheekbones and deep brown-black eyes. She wore a charcoal-gray skirt suit and stood on a platform with a sign in red, white and blue that read VOTE LIGHT-FEATHER FOR CONGRESS. She was a beautiful woman who held her head high and proud, with determination in her gaze.

Liza looked up from the tablet and met Commander's gaze. "I don't understand."

"This woman is a danger to our country and our way of life as citizens of the United States of America." Commander's eyes narrowed, and his lips pulled back in a menacing snarl. "The only way to cleanse society of people like her is to eliminate the threat."

"Yeah!" Spike pumped his fist in the air.

Commander's gaze never left Liza's.

Her heart sank low in her belly and formed a tight knot. "What do you expect me to do?"

Commander stared straight into her eyes and said in a low, tight tone, "Eliminate the threat."

"How?" she asked.

The fiery intensity of his gaze bore a hole straight through Liza's chest.

Commander finally looked past her to Spike. "Tell her."

"What do you think we've been doing for the past ten months?" Spike demanded. "You've been trained to kill."

Liza shook her head. "You said it was self-defense."

"It is self-defense," Spike insisted. "Self-defense of our country." He grabbed her shoulders and shook her hard. "You've been trained as an assassin. It's time to do your part."

"I'm not an assassin. I can't kill this woman. She's done nothing to me." She shoved the tablet into Spike's chest. "No. I won't. I can't."

Commander spun away and paced the length of the room. "Maybe she's not ready."

"She's ready, I tell you," Spike insisted. "She just needs the right motivation." He gave her one last shake. "You'll perform this mission."

Liza shook her head, horrified at the thought of killing someone. Yes, she'd fought other recruits and the trainers in hand-to-hand combat, but never had she taken it to the extreme, always stopping short of ending her opponent's life.

Spike walked away from her and down the hallway toward the exit.

Liza stood for a moment, her hands gripping the tablet.

Commander faced her, his face a ruddy, angry red. "Our country is fighting a war within. We train people like you to reduce the threat of our nation crumbling from within."

"What about democracy? What about innocent until proven guilty? Don't basic rights matter?" Liza tossed the tablet onto the table and pointed at the woman's photo. "What did she do that makes her so dangerous? Run for a government office? Is it because she's a Native American that she makes you feel threatened? Or because she's a female?"

The ten months of captivity, walking on eggshells and trying to stay alive to protect her daughter all came to a head. Liza couldn't stop herself, even knowing she would pay a price for her disobedience. "Who the hell are you to anoint yourself judge, jury and executioner?"

Commander backhanded Liza so hard she slammed into the wall behind her, her head hitting hard. Gray fog crept into her vision and nearly blinded her to Spike reentering the room.

"She'll do whatever the hell we tell her," Spike

said. He pulled his arm from behind him, dragging Tayla out before him.

Tayla's eyes widened. "Mommy!" she cried and tried to break free of Spike's grip.

"Tayla." Liza fought back the dizziness and pushed away from the wall. Fear gripped her insides so tightly she struggled to breathe.

Commander stared from Liza to Tayla and back, his lips curling. "Damn right, she will."

"You want to keep your brat?" Spike asked.

"Please," Liza said, barely able to push air past her vocal cords.

Commander crossed his arms over his chest. "Then you know what you have to do." He pushed the tablet toward her.

"Mommy?" Tayla's brow furrowed.

"You'll do it," Spike said.

Liza stared at her beautiful little girl and nodded. Tears burned her eyes, but she wouldn't let even one fall.

Spike sneered, his mouth turning up in an evil smile. "You leave first thing in the morning for your assignment. You'd better get a good night's sleep. We'll take good care of the brat until you get back."

"Let me have her for the night. Please," Liza begged.

Spike's eyes narrowed.

"Let her." Commander tipped his chin toward

Tayla. "It'll be a poignant reminder of what's waiting for her upon successfully completing her mission."

"Right." Spike swung Tayla toward Liza. "One last night with the brat should make her more certain of her priorities."

Tayla fell into Liza's arms and clung to her.

"I'll take those." Spike motioned toward the pouch of knives strapped to her thigh. "We'll outfit you in the morning with everything you'll need for the assignment."

She untied the pouch and handed it to Spike. Then she shifted her child and held her close. "It's okay, baby," she lied.

Nothing was okay. How could anything be okay?

To keep her daughter alive, she had to kill a stranger.

CHAPTER 2

Liza left the TOC, carrying Tayla in her arms, blinded by the tears filling her eyes and the onset of dusk. She didn't see someone beside her until a hand reached out, snagged her arm and yanked her into the darker shadows of one of the storage buildings.

Still holding onto Tayla, Liza couldn't defend herself. Thankfully, she didn't have to.

PJ stood in front of her. "You got an assignment, didn't you?" She spoke in hushed tones.

Liza nodded, unable to swallow past the lump lodged in her throat. She glanced around, searching for security cameras.

PJ shook her head. "Their cameras can't find us here." PJ tipped her head toward Tayla, who'd buried her face in Liza's neck. "She's their insurance policy?"

Liza nodded again.

"Mommy," Tayla whispered. "What's an insurance policy?"

"Shhh, baby. I'll tell you later." When she was old enough to understand. "Have you had an assignment?"

PJ nodded. "One."

Liza's eyes widened. "Did you—"

PJ's eyes narrowed in the shadows. "They think I did. Only my target had a traffic accident before I even got to him. I claimed it. They bought it. I passed their test." She shrugged. "Who did you get?"

Liza wasn't sure she should share anything with anyone in The Camp. She didn't know whom she could trust and who might be an insider working for the trainers and Commander. But what did it matter? She had to kill someone to keep her daughter alive. "She's a Native American who ran for Congress."

PJ snorted. "Female. Native American. A threat to their male-dominated, racist beliefs."

"How can I do this?" Liza shook her head. "I can't even step on a bug without cringing."

"You're not going to do it," PJ said, her tone matter-of-fact.

"I'm not?" Liza's arms tightened around Tayla. "If I don't..." She bit her bottom lip. "She's...my reason for living." Her voice trailed off.

"We're going to get you out of here."

"I leave first thing in the morning. I don't have time to figure out an escape. And you know what happened to the last guy who tried. I can't go without..." she tipped her head toward Tayla, "and I can't put her at risk."

"Mommy, are you going to leave me?" Tayla's hand curled into Liza's shirt. "Please, don't leave me."

"Oh, baby," Liza pressed her lips against Tayla's soft hair.

"Your Mommy's not going to leave you." PJ patted Tayla's back, staring into Liza's gaze as she did. "We'll figure it out. In the meantime, go get something to eat. You're in luck; I hear they added venison to the vegetable stew. Are you hungry, Tayla?"

Tayla nodded, her gaze wary.

"Yes, baby, let's get you something to eat." Liza wasn't hungry anymore. She was sick to her stomach at the thought of having to kill.

"You two go. I'll follow in a minute." She pointed up. "They'll be watching."

Liza nodded. Still holding Tayla, she stepped out of the shadows and hurried toward the mess hall, her thoughts spinning.

How was PJ going to get her and Tayla out of the compound? If they caught them, they'd kill Liza for sure. But what would happen to Tayla? Would they kill her? Or would they keep her and raise her to be an assassin?

Dear, sweet Lord don't make my baby an assassin.

Before entering the chow hall, Liza set Tayla on her feet and took her hand. "Are you okay?"

Tayla nodded and squeezed Liza's fingers.

Her heart swelled, and more tears welled in her eyes. She blinked them back, squared her shoulders and marched into the building. She put on her best poker face, grabbed a tray and went through the food line.

If she was leaving, she might have to hide in the woods and run. A lot. Carrying Tayla. Her daughter was small. She wouldn't get far at her pace.

Though she wasn't sure how she'd pack it in, she loaded her tray with two bowls of venison stew and two slices of bread and headed for an empty table in the far corner. She couldn't take more food without being noticed. The guards counted every slice of bread.

Recruits weren't allowed to talk among themselves in the chow hall. Guards ate with them and yelled if anyone so much as whispered.

Once, someone sneezed, and another person automatically said, "Bless you." The guards made all the recruits dump the food on their plates into the compost pile and leave the mess hall.

Liza set the tray on the table and placed Tayla's bowl and bread in front of her. She didn't have to say anything to her daughter. The little girl had gone hungry on several occasions. She didn't pick at her food but ate solemnly until she was full.

Liza forced the food down her throat. It was fuel

for her body and what might lie ahead. She even ate what was left in Tayla's bowl.

When they were finished, she carried their tray into the kitchen, washed their dishes and stacked them in a drying rack.

By the time they left the mess hall, night cloaked the compound, with only dim lights on the corners of a few buildings to light their way back to the bunkhouse. Those lights would be turned off by nine o'clock when all the recruits were supposed to sleep. Their days started early at five o'clock.

Liza made a quick stop at the latrine and helped Tayla in and out of her jeans. She'd grown so much over the past ten months that the jean's legs were too short and the button hard to manage. They were getting so snug.

Tayla pushed Liza's hands away. "I can do it myself."

Liza's heart hurt for her little girl. At The Camp, everyone had to fend for themselves, including the children. While Liza trained all day, Tayla was in the care of Nyx, one of the female trainers, who made all the children toe the line.

They didn't sit around coloring and playing with toys like most children their age. Nyx, the dark-skinned, black-haired Amazon, who towered over all other women and most of the men in The Camp, led the children through the woods, teaching them about edible plants, where to find water, which berries were poisonous and more.

Older children had two hours of what their trainer called the three Rs—reading, writing and arithmetic. Then they were outside with the adults, in whatever weather, learning how to fight, shoot and throw knives and hatchets. Many afternoons were spent learning how to start fires without matches, how to set up boobytraps and then how to place and detonate explosives.

Tayla buttoned her jeans and walked to the faucet, turned it on and washed her hands and face. They were allowed a shower twice a week in frigid water. Between those times, they bathed what they could beneath the faucet outside the latrine.

Liza watched as others left the mess tent, heading toward the latrines. She searched through the shadowy faces.

PJ hadn't been in the mess hall. If she was going to get Liza out of The Camp, how would she make it happen without letting Liza in on the plan?

Stars filled the sky overhead, shining light in the clear areas not shrouded by trees. Liza looked around the compound as best she could, hoping to catch a glimpse of PJ.

When she'd stalled as long as she could, she took Tayla's hand and walked with her to the building they'd slept in for the duration of their captivity.

The camp's recruits shared the bunkhouse filled with metal-framed bunk beds.

Liza slept on the top bunk, afraid Tayla would roll over in her sleep and fall out.

When Tayla sat on the edge of the bed and bent over to pull off her shoes, Liza placed her hands over Tayla's, leaned close and said, "Leave your shoes on. It will be easier to get up in the morning."

Tayla frowned down at the tennis shoes that had begun pinching her toes. "But they're dirty."

"It's okay." Liza laid Tayla down and tucked her legs, shoes and all beneath the thin sheets and scratchy wool blanket.

"Wait." Tayla reached beneath the sheets, dug in her jeans pocket and brought out a wilted, smashed flower. "It's not as pretty as it was, but I picked it for you." She held out her prize to Liza.

Liza took it from her little fingers and held it close to her heart. "I love it, sweetie. Thank you." She leaned over and pressed her lips to her daughter's forehead. "Sleep well, Tay. I love you."

Tayla wrapped her arms around Liza's neck and held on tightly. "I love you, Mommy." Then she whispered softly, "Don't leave me."

"I won't, baby," Liza promised, wondering how she'd fulfill that promise if she was still there in the morning. "Sleep, baby, and dream of a field full of dandelions."

"Can I dream about a puppy?"

Liza smiled and brushed a strand of hair off her daughter's cheek. "Of course." She pressed a kiss to her forehead.

Tayla twisted over and dug beneath her pillow, pulling out the pinecone she kept hidden there. She'd found a piece of string and had tied it to the cone. When no one was watching, she'd drag it behind her as if she were walking a dog. "Kiss Daisy, goodnight."

Liza chuckled. "Can't let her go to sleep without a kiss." She touched her lips to the pinecone and patted it gently. "Goodnight, Daisy." Tucking the pinecone in beside Tayla, she looked down at her beautiful daughter. "Goodnight, Tayla."

As Liza straightened, Tayla asked, "Can I name my dream puppy Daisy?"

"You can name her anything you want," Liza said softly.

Tayla closed her eyes. "I'm dreaming, Mommy." She yawned and smiled. "My puppy is soft...and... fluffy." Tayla let out a soft sigh and slept.

Liza climbed into the top bunk and lay, fully clothed, on top of the Army-green wool blanket. Though it was chilly in the building, she didn't care. If she had to leave quickly, she didn't want to be tangled in sheets and take precious time to pull on her shoes.

As the other recruits trudged into the bunkhouse and dropped into their bunks, the noise slowly died down. Liza's gaze shot from PJ's empty bunk to the door and the big clock above the door. The clock's hands moved steadily closer to nine o'clock and lights out.

A minute before the clock struck nine, a guard entered the bunkhouse, walked the length of the long room and paused in front of PJ's empty bunk.

Liza's pulse leaped and hammered through her veins. The guard turned to face the others in the room. "Where's PJ?" he demanded.

As the big hand hit the twelve, the door opened and PJ entered, her face pale, with dark circles beneath her eyes. "I'm here," she said weakly. "Was in the latrine." She rubbed her flat belly. "Something didn't sit right with my stomach."

"I don't care. Get your ass in the bed." He poked a finger toward her bunk. "Now."

PJ hurried down the center of the building and dove into her bed, assuming the fetal position, her arms wrapped around her middle.

The guard marched for the door, muttering something about wasting time. When he reached the end, he opened the door, hit the light switch and left, closing and locking the door behind him.

Abject despair filled Liza's soul. Any chance of escape had just been cut off. The door was locked, PJ hadn't come up with a plan and it was too late now to change any of that.

In the darkness, as other recruits settled in for the

night, Liza let go of the tears she'd held back. They slipped silently from the corners of her eyes.

She lay for a long time, staring up at the ceiling, counting the minutes until she had to leave Tayla and go out and kill a stranger.

Liza must have fallen asleep. What seemed like seconds later, a hand clamped over her mouth and another on her arm.

Instantly awake, Liza went into defensive mode. She knocked the hands away from her and turned to look into PJ's face.

The other woman held a finger up to her lips and jerked her head toward the door.

Liza slipped down from the top bunk, landing silently on the floor.

PJ pressed something into her hands. "Put it on," she whispered so quietly only Liza would hear.

The dark pouch was the one PJ had worn earlier. It contained six throwing knives.

Careful not to let the knives bang together, Liza strapped the pouch to her thigh. Then she scooped Tayla up in her arms.

Tayla stirred and reached toward her bed. "Daisy," she whispered.

Liza leaned over.

Tayla grabbed the pinecone and tucked it between her and Liza.

Liza spun and followed PJ to the door.

PJ didn't bother to twist the handle. She pulled

the door open, removed a rock from the latch hole and stuffed it into her pocket.

In the dim light that managed to find its way through the painted windows, Liza looked at the sleeping forms of the others, praying they didn't wake and sound the alarm.

Once outside, Liza glanced up. "What about the cameras?" she asked softly.

"I cut the cable to the satellite internet after Commander and Spike left the TOC and the guards changed shifts. We only have a few minutes before the next shift wakes and notices the comms are down. Come on." She led the way, moving from shadow to shadow across the compound to the motor pool where the trucks and SUVs were parked.

PJ stopped in the shadow of a storage building.

Liza stopped behind her.

Tayla stirred and blinked her eyes open.

Liza pressed her lips to her daughter's ear and whispered, "Sleep, baby. Everything's okay."

Tayla sighed and closed her eyes, laying her cheek on Liza's shoulder.

With Tayla fast asleep, Liza dared to look over PJ's shoulder, wondering why she'd stopped for so long.

Her heart skipped several beats and then pounded hard against her ribs. Liza fought to stay calm.

Two guards leaned against the hood of one of the trucks, smoking cigarettes. Each had on a helmet with night vision goggles perched on the rims. They'd see their heat signatures in the darkness and find Liza and Tayla fast.

This wasn't going to work. Liza almost reached for PJ to tell her they had to go back to the bunkhouse before they were discovered.

Before her hand touched PJ's arm, the other woman turned to Liza, grabbed her by the front of her shirt and leaned her mouth close to Liza's ear. She spoke softly, but every word was articulated as if strung tightly like the strings on a violin. "Be ready to run for that truck. The keys are in it. Put Tayla on the floorboard and drive. Don't look back, stay low behind the wheel and don't stop for anything."

"But those men—" Liza breathed. How would she get past them without being shot?

"They'll be gone in thirty seconds." PJ held up a small device with a button. "Ready?"

Liza's pulse raced, and her breathing became erratic. She had only one chance. If she didn't make it good, her life and Tayla's would be over. Plus, PJ would be compromised for helping.

Liza kissed her baby's cheek and clutched her close. Drawing a deep breath, she willed her nerves to calm like she had before she'd thrown that knife at Tayla.

She met PJ's gaze. "I'm ready. And thank you."

"Don't thank me yet," PJ warned. She raised her hand and pressed the button.

A loud explosion ripped through the night. Flames shot into the air from the other side of the mess hall where the propane tanks were.

Shouts sounded, and people burst from the buildings, running toward the fire.

The guards dropped their cigarettes and ran toward the flames.

"Go." PJ shoved Liza.

She resisted stepping out of the shadows. "What about you? You're coming too, aren't you?"

PJ shook her head. "I'm going back to the bunkhouse before they realize I'm gone. Go!"

Liza ran for the truck.

Tayla woke and clung to her, eyes wide.

When Liza reached the driver's door, she flung it open and shoved Tayla inside. "Get on the floor," she ordered.

Clutching her pinecone in her hand, Tayla slid across the seat and dropped onto the floor. She huddled there, Daisy between her palms.

Liza started to climb in, took one look at the other vehicles lined up nearby and shook her head.

"Don't move," she told Tayla.

Pulling a knife from the pouch on her thigh, she ran to the lead vehicles and jabbed the knife into the front tires. Flat tires wouldn't stop the guards from following her but changing them first would slow them down. Hopefully, enough to let her get a good lead.

Liza climbed into the truck and fumbled to find the key. Her fingers wrapped around cool metal. Just as she was about to start the engine, a guard ran past, carrying a fire extinguisher.

Once he was out of sight, Liza turned the key. The engine rumbled and died. She pumped the gas pedal and turned the key again. This time, the engine turned over, sputtered and then roared to life.

Liza shoved the gear shift into drive and jammed the accelerator to the floor. The truck leaped forward, the tail skidding sideways.

Holding the steering wheel steady, her gaze on the road leading out of the compound, Liza didn't let up on the gas. The truck blasted past the TOC, several of the trainer's quarters and down the long road to the gate. She didn't turn on the lights, relying on the starlight to see where she was going.

As she neared the gate, she didn't slow.

Two guards stepped between her and the gate, holding their rifles at the ready. One held up a hand and shouted, "Halt!"

Liza held her course, hunkering as low as she could get over the steering wheel and still see.

When she was less than twenty yards from the gate, the guards lifted their rifles.

Liza prayed for a miracle as she raced ahead.

They each fired a warning shot over the top of the truck, then lowered their weapons and aimed at her.

"Please be lousy shots," she prayed out loud.

Bullets pierced the windshield just above Liza's head.

She ducked even lower and kept her foot hard against the accelerator.

They fired again and then dove sideways.

Liza flinched as the truck plowed through the chain-link gate, sending poles and fencing flying over the hood. Then she was through.

Shots rang out behind her. Bullets pierced metal somewhere on the truck. Liza didn't dwell on it. As long as the tires and engine were good and neither she nor Tayla was hit, she'd count herself lucky. A tenth of a mile further, the dirt road emerged onto pavement.

Liza slammed on the brakes and spun the steering wheel to the right. She had no idea where she was or which way to go. All she knew was to keep going.

CHAPTER 3

Pierce "Utah" Turner glanced at his watch for the fifth time since he and the rest of his team had arrived at the third bar in their pub crawl.

Drake Morgan clapped a hand on his shoulder and slid another beer in front of him. "What's eating you?"

"Nothing," he said.

"Come on, Utah," Drake said. "You've been staring at your watch all evening. Are you ready to call it a night?"

Pierce didn't even cringe at the nickname he'd been tagged with back in another life. As a member of Marine Force Recon, he'd been assigned to a joint task force to extract a Taliban leader. Alive. Army Intelligence wanted to interrogate him.

When the operation had gone sideways, they'd been pinned down in a small village. Their target had made them his target, raining machine gun rounds down on them from the top of a building.

The other task force members had wanted to fire a grenade launcher at the building or call for fire support to drop a missile, taking out the Taliban leader before he and his machine gun could kill them all.

While the team had debated the kill, Utah had stuck to the original intent of the mission, insisting on going in alone.

One of the Delta Force operators had called out over the radio, "Let the uptight asshole go in. We don't need a UTAH Marine calling the shots. When he gets plugged, we'll send in the big guns to clean up."

Utah had resented the call. The lone Marine among Army Delta Force soldiers and Navy SEALs, he'd gone into the hot zone. While the rest of the team had covered for him, he'd slipped around to the back of the building. He'd scaled the wall, taken out the two men manning the machine gun and captured the Taliban leader they'd been defending.

Once his man was zip-tied, he'd called over the radio, "This uptight asshole has secured the target. Alive. Ready for extraction."

Though he'd proven himself to the Deltas and SEALs and earned their respect, the moniker had stuck. No matter where he'd been assigned, that name had followed him throughout his career—even into his post-military life, working as contracted security for civilian corporations helping to rebuild infrastructure in Afghanistan.

To this team of men, he was Utah. And he was okay with that.

"I'm fine," he assured Drake. "Just going over what I need to do tomorrow."

"That's tomorrow," Judge said. "You're here with us. Be in the moment, man."

"That's right," Michael "Grimm" Reaper said. "We're here to celebrate Murdock's engagement and forthcoming wedding." Grimm lifted his shot glass. "Another one bites the dust of bachelorhood. To Murdock and Gabbie!"

Utah lifted the beer Drake had placed in front of him. "To Murdock." He took a small sip and set the bottle on the bar. The others planned to stay the night in Bozeman.

Utah was heading back to Eagle Rock soon. He'd volunteered to be at the Lucky Lady Lodge early the next morning to meet the party rental company and florist coming up from Bozeman. He'd help with the heavy lifting and directing where everything would go according to Gabbie and Murdock's instructions.

The rest of the team would ensure Murdock made it back to the lodge in time for the wedding at five o'clock that evening.

Why people went to so much trouble for a wedding, Utah didn't understand. But if it was what they wanted and made his friend happy, he would make sure it was done right.

Which meant he wasn't drinking heavily like the others.

As the hour neared midnight, Grimm and Drake found the karaoke machine and sang about friends in low places. Both were off-key, but no one seemed to care.

Joe "Judge" Smith, the old man of the team, stepped up beside Utah. "You should hit the road. The singing is only going to get worse."

Utah chuckled. "Has anyone ever told those two they can't hold a tune?"

Judge shook his head. "Wouldn't do any good. They're determined to butcher that song." He nodded toward Murdock, who sat with his back to the bar, looking a little shell-shocked. "Think he's getting cold feet?"

Utah studied his friend. "I don't know. Let's ask." He called out, "Hey, Murdock. Having second thoughts? You know it's not a done deal until you say *I do*."

Sean Murdock blinked and turned to face Utah with a frown. "No second thoughts about the wedding and marrying Gabbie and the girls." He scrubbed a hand down his face. "My only regret is that last shot of tequila." He pushed to his feet, steadying himself with a hand on the bar. As soon as he let go, his knees buckled.

Utah rushed forward and caught him before he face-planted on the barroom floor.

"I think our groom has had enough," Utah said loud enough to cut through Grimm and Drake's last few strains of the song.

"What?" Grimm frowned. "We still have one more pub to crawl before we call it a night."

"You'll have to go without Murdock." Judge looped the groom's arm over his shoulder and wrapped his arm around the man's back. "It's a good thing the hotel is only a block away. I don't think he can walk any farther, and none of you are sober enough to drive."

Utah didn't even have a buzz. He hadn't finished an entire beer at any of the three places they'd visited that night.

"I can walk," Murdock said. "Just need a little help from my buddy, Judge, here." He swayed.

Judge shot a glance toward Utah. "Go on. You need to get back before it gets any later. We'll get Murdock to the hotel and tuck him in for the night."

"Are you sure?" Utah met Judge's gaze. "I can help get him there."

"I'm solid," Judge assured him. "I only drank two beers all night. You have to wrangle wedding decorations in the morning. I can herd these guys to the hotel."

"Judge is right," Grimm joined them. "We can manage."

"You're going straight to the hotel, right?" Utah pinned Grimm with a hard stare.

Grimm snorted. "You got that uptight-asshole-thing down to a science, don't you?"

Drake chuckled as he draped Murdock's other arm over his shoulder. "Come on, Grimm. We have to get this guy to bed so he can sober up before the wedding tomorrow. Can't have him missing his big day."

Grimm's lips twisted. "Just when I was getting warmed up," he grumbled.

"You three have one job," Utah said. "Get Murdock to the wedding on time. "Can you do that?"

As one, Grimm, Drake and Judge popped a salute.

"On it," Drake said.

"We've got this," Judge seconded.

"Murdock, who?" Grimm concluded and laughed at his own joke.

Utah shook his head. "I'm staying until I know you are all safe in your hotel rooms."

"We don't need a babysitter." Grimm belched and patted his belly. "Too many bubbles in that beer."

Utah turned to the bartender. "Close out my account. These guys are done for the night."

"Party pooper," Grimm said.

"Get me to the church on time," Murdock sang.

"We will," Drake said.

Utah signed the tab and turned to herd his friends through the door. "Come on, guys." He walked with them the one block to the hotel. Yeah, they could have made it on their own, but he would have worried all the way back to Eagle Rock.

Once the elevator reached their floor, the first stop was Murdock's room. Judge and Drake poured him into the bed, removed his shoes and turned off the light on his nightstand.

"Sweet dreams," Utah said.

"I'm getting married tomorrow," Murdock murmured. "Luckiest man alive." He lay with his eyes closed, a smile curving his lips.

Utah waved the others out of the room and closed the door behind him.

After he and Judge got Grimm and Drake to their rooms, Utah finally felt confident enough to leave his friends.

"You're a good man, Utah," Judge said. "I'm calling it a night. Glad I'm not the one driving back to Eagle Rock tonight."

"See you in the morning." Utah grinned. "Or should I say afternoon? Make sure he sleeps off that tequila and gets a good breakfast in him. We want him sober and not hungover by five o'clock."

"I'll make sure it happens." Judge stopped in front of another door. "Three down. It's just you and me holding out as confirmed bachelors."

Utah shrugged. "Haven't met a woman who could make me want to change the status quo. I figure I'm like everyone claims...an uptight asshole. I have no intention of changing."

"Ah, there's someone out there who'll make you want to be a better man."

"Seriously doubt it. You speak as if you've met someone like that." Utah's eyes narrowed. "You've been married before?"

Judge shook his head. "No." He stared past Utah as if looking into the past. "I let one get away."

"Can't you go back and get her?"

He shook his head. "No. She's happily married, has a beautiful family and I wouldn't bust them up. But I learned something. If you find someone you know is right for you, don't let her get away without telling her how you feel. I waited too long."

"You think there's more than one person out there?" Utah asked.

Judge lifted his shoulders and let them fall. "I'll let you know if I find her." He gave a mock salute. "Be careful on that drive back. Don't pick up any hitchhikers."

"Like there would be any hitchhikers on the road to Eagle Rock at this hour." Utah shook his head. "See ya tomorrow."

Judge entered his room and closed the door.

Utah headed for the elevator, rode it down and stepped out into the cool Montana air.

With no clouds in the sky, the temperature had dropped thirty degrees since sundown. Utah shivered, pulled the collar of his coat up and headed for his truck.

He didn't mind the drive back to Eagle Rock. After celebrating with his friends, he was ready for the peace and quiet beauty of Big Sky country.

He drove out of Bozeman, heading for the small town of Eagle Rock, nestled in the Crazy Mountains. The stars overhead shone so brightly he didn't need his headlights to see the road ahead. He considered turning them off but decided against it. Yes, he could see without them, but oncoming traffic might not see him. He couldn't tempt fate when he had a job to do tomorrow.

Halfway to Eagle Rock, the road curved through the foothills, rising over ridges and down into valleys. He drove defensively, keeping watch for animals that came out at night and occasionally wandered across the roads.

At every curve, he slowed, cautious about what might be around the other side. One switchback forced him to slow to a crawl. He increased his speed on the other side. This part of the road had a steep drop-off.

He was glad his friends hadn't attempted to drive back. The highway was treacherous enough at night when a man was sober. It would be deadly if the driver were under the influence.

The next curve took him around a massive bluff on his left with a sheer drop-off on the right. He dared a glance toward the shoulder of the road that fell steeply down into a gully below. When he looked back at the road, he slammed on his brakes and skidded sideways toward that shoulder.

His truck slowed, coming to a stop with his wheels mere inches from the edge.

In front of him was a truck stopped as far over as it could get, but still blocking his side of the road.

"What idiot parks a truck in the middle of a blind curve?" he muttered.

He glanced in his rearview mirror. From where his truck stood, he couldn't see traffic coming from behind. Utah was pretty sure there hadn't been anyone close behind him. Had there been headlights, he would have noticed. That gave him a little time to figure out what to do. He couldn't let this bonehead leave his truck where it was. Someone else might plow into it.

Remembering Judge's warning not to pick up hitchhikers, Utah pulled his gun out of the glove box and dropped down from his truck.

"Hello," he called out.

No one answered.

As he neared the stalled truck, the beam of his headlights caught strange patterns in the vehicle's body.

His pulse quickened, and his senses shifted to high alert.

The truck appeared to be abandoned.

Still, Utah approached slowly, keeping his body turned sideways, providing less of a target.

Bullet holes in the tailgate and a clean hole through the back window didn't bode well for what he might find inside the cab. Whoever had been driving might not have had a choice of where to park.

Bracing himself for being shot at or facing a dead driver, he took a deep breath and peeked around the doorframe into the cab.

Empty.

The front windshield had two bullet holes. As far as Utah could tell, there was no blood in the seat. That was good for the driver. Potentially bad for him.

He could have parked the truck in the road, setting a trap for the first unlucky soul to come across it.

The sound of footsteps in gravel made him duck below the hood and inch around the front of the vehicle.

With the starlight shining brightly overhead, it only took a moment to spot the owner of the feet, making a sad attempt to hide behind a scrawny excuse for a tree. The tree clung to the side of the highway on the only patch of ground standing between the road and the steep ravine that fell sharply to a rocky gully below.

A large boulder rested beside the tree, having fallen from the massive bluff on the other side of the highway at some time since the highway had been built.

From the size of the person hiding behind the tree, Utah guessed it was a female or a very small male. He looked around for any other hiding places. The boulder was too small for the woman to hide behind, much less a man. Nothing else provided a suitable hiding place for anyone else.

Holding his gun out in front of him, he aimed at the shadowy figure behind the tree. "I can see you standing there. You might as well come out."

When she didn't move, he moved closer.

"You collected a few bullet holes in your truck." He kept his tone light and amiable. Hopefully, non-threatening. "If you're in trouble, maybe I can help."

"You can't," a soft voice whispered.

If he hadn't been straining to hear even the slightest sound, he wouldn't have heard her words. "I can't help if I don't know what the trouble is."

"I don't need your help," she said. "Go away."

"Nope," he said. "Not an option. Not until that truck is moved. It's in a bad spot. I was lucky enough to stop in time. The next guy might not be so lucky. Is it operational?"

"Yes."

"Can you move it?" he asked.

"No."

"Why?"

A long stretch of silence followed, and then a sigh before she answered, "Out of gas."

"I could siphon some from my truck to put in yours. Enough to get you into Eagle Rock, where you can fill up."

"No. I can't. I don't have any money." She remained behind the tree, nothing but a shadowy figure with a soft, scared voice.

"I can give you some. Enough to get you to where you're going."

She snorted at his words.

Utah walked closer. "At the very least, we need to push the truck out of the curve and off the side of the road. I can push if you'll drive."

"Why should I trust you?" she asked.

"Because I'm one of the good guys?" Frustrated, he took another step closer. "Look, you don't have many choices, and that truck needs to move before it gets someone killed."

For a long moment, she remained still, tucked behind the tree.

When he thought he'd have to move the truck himself, she finally stepped around the tree and stood before him in the starlight.

She wore jeans and a jacket that couldn't be warm enough for the nearly freezing temperature. Her hair was pulled back behind her head. She was thin, with dark shadows beneath her eyes, giving her a haunted appearance.

"I really am one of the good guys," he said. "At least, trust me long enough to get the truck off the highway. I won't even ask you about the bullet holes."

"I'll drive if you'll push." She tipped her chin toward the gun in his hand. "I can't attack you if I'm sitting in the cab."

"Fair enough," he said and tucked the Glock into the waistband of his jeans. "Get in, put it in neutral and steer it around the curve. I'll push until we find a place to safely park it off the road."

He returned to the bullet-ridden vehicle, wondering what this woman had gone through. He didn't blame her for being cautious. One of the bullet holes had gone through the windshield a few inches above the steering wheel. How had it not hit her?

He stopped when he reached the tailgate.

Only then did the woman approach the truck and climb into the driver's seat. She pressed the brake and shifted into neutral.

"Ready?" he called out.

"Ready," she responded and let off the brake.

Utah leaned all his weight into the tailgate, digging his feet into the pavement.

The truck rolled slowly, picking up speed to a point where Utah wasn't pushing anymore. He ran along behind it, hoping the woman was looking ahead for a safe place to park it.

Suddenly, the truck swerved to the right. The

driver's door opened at the same moment the front tires flew over the shoulder.

"Holy shit." Utah ran toward the truck but could do nothing to stop it from pitching over the side of the hill and plummeting down the steep incline, crashing into the boulders below.

He ran to the edge of the road and stared at the mangled hunk of metal, wondering how he could safely get down the sheer drop-off without rappelling gear. The thought of the woman trapped in the smashed cab made him throw caution to the wind.

About to step over the edge and figure it out on the way down, a voice nearby stopped him.

"Don't," she called out weakly. "I got out. But I need a little help."

"What the hell?" He found her lying on the ground, her hands wrapped around a stub of a tree and the rest of her body dangling over the side.

Utah edged toward her, the ground around that tree crumbling.

She clung to the tree with both hands, her body trembling with the effort.

"Can you reach up with one hand?" he asked.

Slowly, she released one hand, her body shifting. More dirt and gravel slipped beneath her. When she raised her hand, he knew he had to be quick or risk losing her to the same fate as the bullet-ridden truck.

When her hand was within his reach, he grabbed

past her wrist and leaned back hard at the same time the tree broke free of its roots.

For a moment, Utah teetered, off balance. To keep from tipping over the edge, he fell backward, yanking her up at the same time.

He landed flat on his back with the woman sprawled across his chest. She didn't weigh much, but he couldn't breathe.

For a long moment, he lay with his arms wrapped around her, catching the breath that had been knocked from his lungs.

When she struggled to get up, he released his hold.

She staggered to her feet and ran back the way they'd come, heading for his truck.

Damn. He'd left his keys in it.

Utah rolled to his feet and raced after her.

As the woman came abreast of the boulder and tree Utah had found her hiding behind, he caught up and tackled her.

"What the hell are you doing?" she choked out.

He lay on top of her, holding her down. "That's my truck. You can't have it."

"I don't want your truck," she said, her voice breathy. "Get off me."

He stood and pulled her to her feet, holding onto her wrist to keep her from bolting again.

She tugged at her arm. When he refused to let go, she twisted around behind him. Taking his wrist with her, she shoved it up between his shoulder blades. "I thought you said you were one of the good guys."

"I am. But I couldn't let you steal my truck."

"Like I said, I don't want your damned truck," she bit out.

"Then why did you run toward it?" he asked, standing on his toes to ease the pain she was inflicting on his arm. "Ease up, will you?"

She reached around his waist and grabbed the gun. Before he had time to react, she shoved him forward, releasing his arm as she did.

He spun to face her, his gaze zeroing in on the Glock pointed at his chest. "Now, who's the bad guy?"

The woman lifted her chin, dirty from clinging to the side of the cliff and from having him tackle her to the ground. "You. As far as I can tell."

"If you weren't going for my truck, why were you running?" he demanded.

"Mommy?" a small voice called out behind Utah.

Utah spun toward a tiny, golden-haired child peeking from behind the boulder.

Shocked, Utah blinked. No. The aberration was real.

Cold steel pressed into the middle of his back. "Touch her, and I'll blow a hole right through you."

CHAPTER 4

Liza held the gun steady, pressed into the middle of the stranger's back.

He raised his hands. "I won't touch her," he promised.

Liza couldn't trust anyone. That little girl was her life. "Tayla, come here."

Her daughter eased out from behind the rock, her eyes wide, staring at the man between her and Liza.

"Come on, sweetie," she coaxed. "I won't let him hurt you."

Tayla smiled at the man. "He won't hurt me, Mommy. He's one of the good guys."

Liza didn't want to dash the child's hopes, but she couldn't believe everything people told her. "We don't know if he's good or bad since we just met him."

Tayla's brow wrinkled. "He saved you from falling. Doesn't that make him a good guy?"

"The kid has a good point," the man said, his hands still raised. "If I was a bad guy, I would have let you fall."

"Bad guys can do worse than letting a person fall to her death," Liza said softly for only the man to hear. Then louder, she called out, "Tayla, come here."

Tayla gave the man a wide berth and came to stand beside Liza.

"Now what?" the man said. "Are you going to take my truck after all?" He shrugged. "Go ahead. Seems you need it more than I do based on the one you just ditched."

Liza hadn't thought any further ahead than to get to Tayla and ensure her safety.

"Look, I'm going to turn around. You can shoot me if you want, but I need to move my vehicle. Like I said, parking in the middle of a blind curve can be deadly to the next person who comes along."

Liza backed out of the man's reach, the gun leveled on his upper body. She'd learned how to operate a variety of pistols, rifles and shotguns at The Camp during her ten months of training. Her aim was spot on, even with popup targets.

Could she actually shoot this guy?

Her jaw hardened.

If he made even the slightest attempt to harm Tayla, Liza would shoot him without hesitation.

He turned to face her. "Maybe we'd get along better if we introduced ourselves." He held out his hand. "I'm Pierce Turner. My friends call me Utah."

She stared at his hand without taking it. "Why do they call you Utah? Are you from there?"

He dropped his hand, his lips twisting. "Long story. I got the nickname while serving in the Marine Corps. It stuck." He cocked an eyebrow. "Now's when you tell me who you are."

She shook her head. "You don't need to know me."

Utah glanced down at the child. "And you're Tayla." The man gave Liza's daughter a solemn nod. "How old are you, Tayla?"

She held up three fingers. "I'm three. How old are you?"

The man chuckled. "I'm thirty-one."

A violent shiver shook the little girl's body.

Utah frowned. "You're cold." Immediately, he shrugged off his jacket and stepped toward the child.

Tayla's mother moved to block him.

He held out the coat. "I only want to give her this. It's too cold at night for you both to be in the Crazy Mountains without proper clothing." He drew in a deep breath. "Look, let me drive you somewhere. I can't leave you stranded on the highway. If you care about your little girl, you'll let me help."

"I don't trust you," the child's mother said.

"You don't have to. You can keep the gun and shoot me if I make any threatening moves."

Her eyes narrowed.

"I'll take you anywhere you want to go," he offered. "Name it."

"Anywhere?" she asked.

He smiled. "Anywhere I can get to in my truck, that is. How about a hotel? You both look like you could do with a warm place and some sleep in a soft bed."

Tayla's mother shook her head. "I can't."

"If you're short on cash, I'll give you the money. Just make a decision. The longer we stand here, the greater the chance someone will come along and crash into the back of my truck. Do you want someone's death on your conscience?"

Liza winced. "No." She'd made a daring escape from The Camp to avoid the assignment to kill an innocent woman. She waved the gun toward the truck. "Go. Move the truck."

"Only if you and Tayla go with me." He waved a hand. "You can't stay out here in the cold."

Liza couldn't control the shiver that shook her entire frame.

"I'm cold, Mommy," Tayla said, her teeth chattering. "Can't we go with the good guy?"

"I'll take you into Eagle Rock. You can decide what to do from there. If you want me to take you further, I'll do it. In all good conscience, I can't leave you two on the side of the road. You don't know what animals are out here, and you risk hypothermia."

What he said was true. Besides the four-legged animals, there were the two-legged monsters like the ones who'd kidnapped her and Tayla ten months ago and forced her into training to become an assassin.

"Please, Mommy," Tayla whispered.

Tired to her very bones and so cold she could barely hold the pistol straight, Liza heaved a sigh. "Okay. We'll go with you."

"If you need a place to stay, I work at the Lucky Lady Lodge. Unfortunately, many of the rooms are closed due to renovation. The owner might cut you deal on one of the vacant ones."

"I can't pay," Liza said.

"Right...no money." He stared at her. "Fine. Then it can be my treat."

She shook her head before he finished his sentence. "I don't take money from strangers."

He shoved his hand through his hair. "Lady, as far as I can tell, you don't have money or transportation. I won't leave you stranded. It's against my nature. I'm tired and have a wedding to put together in the morning. I'll spot you the money for the room. You can pay me back when you're on your feet and able."

After a long moment, where she weighed her options and couldn't think of anything better, she said, "Okay."

He glanced at her as if he didn't quite believe

she'd capitulated. "Well…good." Again, he held out the coat. "Can Tayla have this before she turns into an icicle?"

Tayla looked up at Liza, her gaze imploring her mother to let her have the coat.

"Yes." She tightened her grip on the gun, her fingers stiff from the chill in the air. "No funny business."

He gave her a tight smile. "There's nothing funny about freezing your ass off in the Crazy Mountains with a woman who argues about everything," he grumbled. Utah dropped to a squat and held the jacket open. It was big enough to wrap around the little girl twice, covering her from her neck to her toes.

Tayla let him wrap it around her and smiled up at him. "See, Mommy? He's a good guy."

The jury was still out in Liza's mind. Other than her father, she hadn't met many men she could trust. Then again, coming from the small town of Valier, Montana, she hadn't met many men.

The trainers and the recruits at The Camp were all lumped into the Do Not Trust category. Though most of the recruits had been kidnapped like her and Tayla, they'd been brainwashed by punishment and events to rat on each other if anyone stepped out of line.

Utah straightened. "Now, I'm going to walk to the truck. You can keep pointing that gun at me or not. I don't care. Just get in. It's going to be morning before you know it."

Liza shot a worried glance at the sky. She needed to get out of the open before too many people saw her. She wasn't sure how far and wide the group who'd kidnapped her extended. Did they have a network of informants throughout Montana? Did their network expand past the state's borders into Wyoming, Idaho and Washington?

She'd heard the trainers talking about the group. They'd referred to it as TCW. She'd never heard them discuss what the letters stood for. As far as she was concerned, she didn't want to know and would stay as far away from them as possible.

Another shiver shook her entire body, forcing her to make a decision she didn't want to make. Like he'd pointed out...she didn't have much choice.

If she insisted on him leaving without her and Tayla, they might not see another vehicle pass on the highway until morning. If one did happen by, she couldn't know if the driver was from The Camp, knew about TCW or was just a bad guy bent on taking advantage of a woman and her small child.

Liza bent to lift Tayla with her empty arm but couldn't get a good grip with only one hand and the bulk of Utah's coat to maneuver around. So, she shifted the gun to her left hand and tried again, failing miserably.

"For the love of fudge." Utah brushed her hand

aside, scooped Tayla up in his arms and deposited her into the back seat of his pickup.

Liza held the gun on him, fear stabbing through her heart. What if he knocked her out and took off with Tayla?

Utah buckled the seatbelt across the child's lap, shut the door and opened the front passenger door. "You know, she's so small, she really needs a car seat." He nodded to the interior. "You're up. It would be a lot easier if you put the gun down."

"No way," she said.

He shrugged. "Have it your way."

He stood by, waiting for Liza to climb up into the truck.

With the gun back in her right hand, she tried holding the door frame to pull herself up onto the running board. With no handle to hold, her fingers slipped. Liza fell backward and would have landed flat on her ass if Utah hadn't caught her beneath her arms.

As quickly as he caught her, he set her on her feet, his hands resting on her arms until she was steady. Then he shook his head. "We have to get moving."

Without warning, he scooped her up, much like he had Tayla and deposited her in the passenger seat.

When Utah reached across her to buckle her seatbelt, Liza protested. "I'm not a child. I can do this myself." She immediately realized the irony of her words…the same words Tayla had used when she'd buttoned her own jeans.

"I know you can do it yourself—but not with a gun in one hand. If you insist on holding that thing, you'll need help with everything else. Just so you know, I'll want that gun back before we part ways."

Liza had never liked guns before her abduction. Especially when she was on the other end of the barrel. However, having his gun in her hands gave her some sense of protection. No doubt, she'd give it back, but she'd feel naked and defenseless without it.

The truth was, he could have taken it from her at any time. She was beyond exhausted, both physically and emotionally. Another failure in the eyes of her trainers. Emotion should be left out of any equation.

Emotion got you killed.

As Utah rounded the front of the truck, Liza spun in her seat to look back at Tayla.

Her daughter had slumped against the door, the voluminous coat a blanket and pillow all in one. She was fast asleep, warm and feeling safe with the "good guy."

Liza wished she could feel as warm and safe. But she couldn't trust anyone. Not even the man who'd saved her from falling to the bottom of a steep and rocky ravine. She'd live to see another day and continue to look out for Tayla.

She'd thought of going to the police or sheriff's department to let them know about The Camp and the people who'd been stolen from their homes and families. Some of the kids had been stolen from foster families. Would anyone try hard to find them? Would they care? Those were the ones who had been easily brainwashed, finally having a place where they belonged and could excel at something.

Liza laid the handgun across her lap.

Utah slipped behind the wheel, closed the door and shifted into drive. He glanced in his rearview mirror. "Damn," he muttered and jammed his foot on the accelerator.

Liza glanced over her shoulder. A beam of light shined around the curve in the road. A vehicle shot into the open, roaring around the bend.

Had they remained where they were parked for a moment longer, the oncoming vehicle would have slammed into the back of Utah's truck.

Bright headlights glared, lighting the interior of the cab.

Liza ducked low in her seat. What if the guards, Spike or Commander had caught up with her? Her heart hammered hard in her chest.

She turned her face toward Utah.

He squinted at the bright light blinding him in the rearview mirror. "Dim your lights, dude," he muttered and adjusted the rearview mirror to deflect the glare from hitting him in the eyes.

Utah drove the highway, winding along the curvy road, going slower than Liza would have liked. Then again, she couldn't see what he was seeing or dealing with.

When the road finally straightened, the vehicle behind them roared around them, matched their pace for a few seconds and then shot around Utah's truck.

Once they'd passed, Liza sat up straight and watched as the taillights disappeared around yet another sharp bend.

"Look, you're obviously running from someone?" Utah glanced her way. "Who is he? An abusive boyfriend or husband?"

Liza shook her head slowly. "No boyfriend. Never married."

"A drug dealer you stole money from?"

She frowned. "I have a daughter. I don't do or sell drugs."

"If I'm going to help you, I need to know who you're scared of—who to watch for. Who you're running from?"

She turned away, staring at the window and her reflection looking back at her. Utah's face was there as well. He wouldn't stop asking until she told him something. Why not the truth? "I'm running from people who abducted Tayla and me ten months ago."

"Jesus," Utah said, lifting his foot from the accelerator. "Why did you ditch your truck?"

"It wasn't my truck," she said. "I stole it. They might have a tracker on it. They could follow me. I only needed it to get as far as I could before we abandoned it." She gave him a crooked smile. "Thank you for helping me hide."

His lips pressed into a thin line. "You could have warned me before almost going over the edge with it."

"I didn't think you would be keen on the idea."

"Are the people who abducted you the same ones who put the bullet holes in the truck?"

Liza nodded, her gut clenching again as images of the guards at the gate flashed through her memory like an action-adventure or thriller movie. The other memory echoing through her thoughts was of Commander standing before all the recruits and trainers after they'd brought Teej's body back into the compound. Commander had stared at the people gathered, his eyes narrowed, his face set in stone. "No one escapes. No. One."

She hadn't realized she'd repeated the words aloud until Utah responded, "But you did."

"Yeah, until they find us."

"Who are these people?" Utah asked.

Liza gave a bark of laughter. "I don't know who they are. We weren't allowed to call them by their given names. They used nicknames or callsigns. My trainer was Spike. The man in charge of The Camp was Commander. They called me Fly."

"Fly?" Utah's brow dipped. "Why?"

Liza shrugged. "I don't know," she lied. She knew

they'd called her Fly because of her skill at throwing knives. She could make them fly through the air with the smoothest and deadliest precision. She still wore the pouch tied to her thigh. Her long jacket covered the knives. She was surprised Utah hadn't felt them when he'd pulled her up from the cliff or when he'd scooped her up and sat her in the passenger seat of his truck.

Utah frowned. "You need to take this to the police.

Liza shook her head. "They can't know where I am. If I go to the police, they'll know where I am. They'll find Tayla and me. They have a network across the whole state of Montana. Probably even into neighboring states. They're watching. Someone will find out I've leaked information about the compound. They'll come for us."

Liza shook her head. "I can't let them find me. I sure as hell can't let them find Tayla."

"Well, if your name isn't Fly, what *is* your name?"

She snorted softly. "It doesn't matter. That person no longer exists. She was wiped off the face of the earth ten months ago."

Utah slapped his hand on the steering wheel. "It damned sure does matter. And you're still the same person you were before this started. Just more... seasoned." He gave her a gentle smile. "Tell me your name. Your family deserves to know you're alive."

She laughed. "The only family I have is here in the truck."

He looked at her sharply. "What about your parents?"

"Dead," she said, her tone flat. Emotionless. Spike would have been proud. Not that she gave a damn about the man who'd made her life miserable and then forced her to throw a knife at her daughter. He could rot in hell for all she cared.

"Siblings?" Utah pressed.

"None," she replied.

His mouth twisted. "We have that in common. I'm an only child."

"I wasn't an only child," Liza said. "My older brother died in Syria. He was in the Army. It broke my father's heart. He wasn't the same after they brought Ryan home in a box."

"I'm sorry," he said softly. "What about Tayla's father? Doesn't he care to know his daughter is alive and well?"

"Ha," Liza said. "She doesn't exist to Nathan. He doesn't exist to her. I prefer it that way. It's better than having to explain to Tayla that she has a deadbeat father who never wanted her and would never visit. Better to have no dad at all."

Utah nodded. "You and Tayla are on the run, but you can't hide forever. If you take this information to the police or sheriff and lead them back to where they held you captive, they can shut them down."

She leveled a tight gaze at Utah. "What part of they have people everywhere do you not understand? I don't know how many training sites they have all over the region. One of those sites was overrun recently. They just moved to others. Some of their people came to the compound where we were being held. These people are like ants. You take them out in one location, and they'll pop up in another." Her hands curled into fists. "And they don't just let you leave. I guarantee that they're looking for me now."

"Okay, okay. So, you don't want to notify the police. What about a private company that can keep your whereabouts confidential?"

Liza shook her head. "I have to lay low to protect Tayla. That little girl is all I have. And I'm all she has."

Utah stared straight ahead, his thumb tapping against the steering wheel. For a long moment, he didn't say anything.

Liza was glad. She was done answering questions and needed time to think about what she would do next and where she and Tayla would go.

Finally, Utah turned toward her. "Let me help."

When Liza opened her mouth to protest, he held up one hand.

"At least for one night. We can consider options tomorrow."

She shook her head. "What was it you said earlier? You have a wedding to prepare?"

Utah muttered a curse under his breath. "You're

right. I can't believe I forgot. But I promise that after the wedding, I can give you my undivided attention. We can figure out some kind of game plan."

Liza's heart warmed at the thought of this man, who didn't know anything about them, offering to help them. Part of her wondered what was in it for him. "You're not responsible for what happens to Tayla and me."

"That's where you're wrong," Utah shot back.

"How so?"

"Have you never heard that when a man saves another person's life, he's responsible for that person from that point forward?" He poked his thumb toward his own chest. "I saved your life. Therefore, I have to make sure nothing happens to you or Tayla."

"That's a slick line of bullshit you're spreading." She turned in her seat to face him. "You don't know us. You don't owe me anything. If anything, I owe you my life. Why are you doing this?"

He shook his head back and forth, his lips curling in a sardonic grin. "Damned if it's because of who I am."

She stared at him, her brow puckering. "I don't understand."

"After ten years in the military, I left and went into private security, guarding contractors in Afghanistan. When I was done with that gig, I swore I wouldn't go back into any kind of protection service. I came to Eagle Rock to shoot nails, not bullets. I was hired to help with the renovations of the Lucky Lady Lodge. I even turned down a job with a damned good protective service that provides security to individuals who need it. I didn't want to go into that line of work. I came to work with my hands and rebuild a lodge."

Liza frowned. "Then why do you feel like you have to provide our security?"

Utah laughed. "I can't get away from it. It's who I am. When someone is in trouble, I can't stand by and do nothing. And sweetheart, it sounds like you and your little girl are in a whole heap of trouble."

Liza stared ahead as they approached a town.

"That's Eagle Rock," Utah said. "We have to pass through and head out the other side to get to the lodge."

Her pulse increased the closer they came to the sleepy little town. Before they passed beneath the glow of streetlights, Liza ducked low. The people who lived there might be asleep, but she couldn't be sure. Better to err on the side of being too cautious than to show her face to a potential member of her captors' network.

Utah slowed as they entered town and traversed the length of Main Street. From what she could see from her crouched position, the town was quaint, with a tavern, the usual banks and a real estate office. It didn't take long to go from the southernmost point of town to the northernmost. Then they left the streetlights behind and continued until they reached a road to the left. Flanked on either side by overhanging trees, the path wound through a forest.

Soon, the trees thinned and eventually opened to a clearing with a huge mountain at one end and an old-time lodge perched against the side of the mountain's rocky edifice.

"That's her," Utah said with pride in his voice. "We've been working on the Lady for the past few months. The renovations are nearing completion. Most of what's left to do is in some of the guest rooms and a couple of the meeting rooms."

"We?" she asked.

"Me and my team." Utah grinned. "You'll meet them tomorrow."

Liza shook her head. "I'm serious, the fewer people who see me, the less likely someone will either intentionally or unintentionally say something about the woman and her small daughter who showed up in the middle of the night."

Utah nodded. "I could introduce you as my cousin or something, who came in for Murdock's wedding. It might throw off the network of informants."

Liza's brow knit. She wanted to take Tayla and disappear. With no money and no transport, she didn't see how that could happen. Her head hurt, and she was so tired her thoughts were nothing more than a murky fog. She pinched the bridge of her nose.

Utah reached across the console and touched her arm. "Don't think about it now. We'll get in late enough that no one will see you enter the lodge. You and Tayla can stay in my room until morning. I'll find somewhere else to sleep."

She looked down at his hand, gently touching her arm and tried to remember the last time someone had been kind to her.

Her eyes burned, but she refused to cry. The situation was tough, but she'd learned to be tougher. Tayla needed a mama bear willing to fight to protect her from harm.

Her little girl also needed a safe place to sleep.

Sleep… As tired as Liza was, how could she sleep knowing Commander, Spike and their entire network would be looking for her and Tayla?

If Utah really was one of the good guys, could she trust him long enough to get some sleep?

CHAPTER 5

Utah parked on the far end of the Lucky Lady Lodge's parking lot, away from the front lobby.

The building's 1800s charm always made him proud of the work he was doing inside. Restoring such a beautiful structure gave him a lot more satisfaction than shooting evil terrorists. Although, ridding the world of terrorists had been rewarding.

He glanced across at Fly and shook his head. "You really need to tell me your name. Otherwise, I'll be forced to call you Fly or Tayla's Mama."

She drew in a deep breath and let it out slowly. "This place is beautiful," she said. "A place I would love to come to for a vacation, not to hide out in case someone sees me and reports back to Commander." She turned to face him. "Liza. My name is Liza." Her hand rose to cover her mouth. "That felt weird to share even that little bit about myself. I had the distinct urge to look over my shoulder to see if anyone overheard me."

"You really didn't share names with others?"

Liza shook her head. "Punishment was harsh. I was horsewhipped for speaking out against my trainer when he slapped one of the women so hard he knocked her down."

Utah's hands tightened around the steering wheel, rage firing through his system. "Jesus, Liza, we need to notify law enforcement. These people need to be stopped."

Liza glanced over her shoulder at her daughter without saying another word.

"Okay. We won't talk about your options until the morning when you both have had a chance to sleep."

"And you've set up for a wedding," she said softly.

The wedding. How had he let himself get talked into helping?

Because he was the only one with any sense of style among his friends. He'd had his mother to thank for that. She'd been an interior designer and had dragged him around to many of her client's homes and offices when he'd been a kid.

An only child, he'd spent more time with adults than other children. He really didn't know what to do with kids, and even less with babies. Hell, he'd never thought about having any of his own. Anytime he was around friends with little ones of their own, he felt awkward. What did he have to say to a small boy or girl?

He looked at the sleeping child in the back seat. Thankfully, her mother was there to take care of her.

Liza stared at the building in front of her. "Are there security cameras?"

Utah nodded. "A brand-new system was installed just last week."

"Is it tied to the internet?"

"I believe so."

She chewed on her bottom lip. "How good is the firewall to keep someone from hacking into the system?"

"I don't know." He reached behind her seat, fished a ball cap out of the pocket and handed it to her. "If you're worried about being picked up on the cameras, wear this and keep your head down. The cameras are on the corners of the building. I don't think anyone will be awake now, looking out the window—but just in case, you'll be covered."

She gave him a weak smile. "Thanks." She tucked her blond braid into the cap and pulled it down low on her forehead, making her look like a young boy instead of the mother of a three-year-old. "How's this?" she asked, looking up at him, her blue eyes round.

Something about her hit him square in the gut. She was too damned cute.

He frowned. "It'll work. Let's get inside. Morning

will be here before we know it." Utah pushed open his door and dropped down from the pickup. He rounded the front to the passenger side.

Liza still sat in the truck, staring at the building.

He opened her door. "It's going to be okay," he said. "Look, I trust everyone who lives and works here with my life."

"That's you," she said softly. "For the past ten months, I've been with people who would just as soon end my life and threaten Tayla's to get me to do what they want. That gives me some real trust issues."

Utah nodded. "I get that. And you don't know me from Adam." He held up his fingers like a Boy Scout. "But I promise—"

"I know," she cut in. "You're one of the good guys."

He grinned. "True, but that's not what I was going to say. I promise to look after you and Tayla. I don't expect you to trust me. But I'm thinking that little girl needs a warm bed and a decent night's sleep. I don't know much about kids. I'm betting that what you two have been through will leave its mark."

Liza pressed a hand to her chest. "That's what I'm afraid of. The best I can do is get her somewhere safe and let her know she's loved."

Utah held out his hand.

Liza hesitated, then laid her palm in his.

"Hang onto the gun," he reminded her.

Her cheeks heated as she grabbed the weapon with her other hand.

Utah fought back a smile. He could have taken that gun from her several times, but if it made her feel safer, she could have it.

He helped her to the ground and then carefully opened the back door, knowing Tayla had been leaning against it. He unbuckled the seatbelt and gathered the wad of child and bulky jacket into his arms.

Liza held out her hands. "I'll take her."

Utah shook his head. "Let me," he said. "I'm just going to carry her inside. You'll be right next to me, holding the gun. I'm not going to steal her away or hurt her." He glanced toward the end of the building. "If you don't want the cameras to pick up the fact you're holding a gun, you might want to tuck it into your pocket."

Liza shoved the pistol into her pocket, keeping her hand inside with it.

She didn't look happy he was carrying her daughter in his arms. He tried to look at everything from her point of view. Hell, he was a stranger. Why would she be comfortable or happy about it? For all she knew, he could be leading her into yet another nightmare, like the one she'd escaped.

Remembering the bullet holes in the truck she'd driven off the road, Utah was amazed she'd made it out alive. It had to have taken a huge amount of courage to make a run for it.

As she turned toward the building, Liza looked up at the sign and read the words "Lucky Lady Lodge." She snorted softly. "What are the chances my luck has changed?"

"You're here, aren't you?" Utah said. "It has to be better than where you were."

She nodded. "I hope so."

Utah led the way to a side entrance with a porch light shining down on the stoop. Clutching Tayla in one arm, he rummaged in his back pocket for his wallet and the key card inside. He caught the corner of his wallet, pulled it from his pocket and immediately dropped it on the ground.

Liza bent to retrieve it. When she straightened, she tried to hand the wallet to him.

"Grab the key card," Utah said. "It's the bright green one with a big clover on it."

Liza riffled through his wallet, extracted the green key card and ran it through the reader on the door lock. A little green light blinked on. She quickly turned the handle and held the door open.

Utah entered, carrying the little child. He noted that Liza no longer had her hand in the pocket with the gun. It was a small step toward trust. He'd take it as a win.

Once they were both inside, Utah led the way through the corridors to the one where he and his teammates had been housed for the duration of the renovations.

Two of the team had moved out of the lodge and in with their fiancées. Though Grimm had found his own lady love, Dezi Thomas, she too lived at the lodge and worked as the restaurant's chef. He'd spent more time in her room than his.

After the wedding, Murdock would move in with his wife in Eagle Rock, where she had a thriving mobile veterinarian business.

Utah wasn't worried about waking anyone because the guys were still in Bozeman, sleeping off the effects of Murdock's bachelor party. From what he'd heard, the women had planned a sleepover at the bride Gabbie Myer's place.

With the renovation still in progress, the owners, Molly and Parker Bailey, had limited the number of guests. Most of the guests staying that night were wedding guests, there for Murdock and Gabbie's nuptials. They were in the newly remodeled rooms in another corridor.

Utah stopped in front of his door and nodded toward the card reader.

Liza ran the card through the locking mechanism and pushed the door open.

"Excuse the clutter. It's been a busy week getting ready for the wedding."

"How long have they been planning for it?" Liza stood to the side.

Utah carried Tayla through the door, a crooked smile on his lips. "This week."

"One week?" Liza shook her head. "That's not enough time to plan a wedding."

"Tell me about it," he said as he laid Tayla on the bed and unwrapped his coat from around her like peeling the tortilla off a burrito.

Her arms were so small and thin. "How did such a tiny creature survive in your camp?"

"She might be little, but she's fierce."

He looked up at Liza. "Like her mother."

Liza shrugged. "We did what we had to do to survive."

"Mommy?" Tayla's eyes blinked open.

"Hey, sweetie." Liza smiled at her daughter. "It's nighttime. Go to sleep, baby."

Tayla looked up at her mother with droopy eyes. "Where's Daisy, Mommy?"

"Oh, baby," Liza said, her eyes sad. "I'm so sorry. Daisy's gone."

The little girl's eyes clouded, and a tear slipped down her cheek. "I loved Daisy."

"Me, too, baby," Liza said. "We'll get you another Daisy soon. I promise."

A second tear slipped down Tayla's cheeks. She closed her eyes. Her breathing grew deeper. Tayla slept.

"Who's Daisy?" Utah asked.

"Tayla's imaginary puppy. It was a pinecone on a

string." Liza brushed a tear from her own cheek. "She loved Daisy. And now Daisy is at the bottom of a cliff in the truck."

"A pinecone? I don't get it." Utah shook his head and stepped back. "This is your thing. Let me get a few things, and then I'll leave you two alone to get some sleep."

Liza stepped up to the bed and removed Tayla's worn shoes, laying them on the floor in front of the nightstand. She brushed a strand of hair back from her daughter's face and rubbed at a spot of dirt on her cheek.

Utah couldn't look away. The tenderness with which Liza touched her daughter tugged at his heart. She'd risked so much to get the two of them out of a terrible situation.

"She needs a bath," Liza glanced up, her gaze meeting his.

Utah realized he'd been staring. "Don't worry about the sheets. I can get them changed with fresh ones after the wedding." He turned toward the other door in the room and pushed it open. He waved a hand toward the adjoining bathroom within. "You'll find fresh towels in the cabinet below the sink and spare toiletries like toothbrushes, toothpaste and a comb." He grabbed his sleeping bag from the far corner of the room and headed toward the hall.

Liza followed, a frown pulling her eyebrows into a V. "Where will you be?"

He shrugged. "I'll find a sofa in the lobby."

Her frown deepened. "Can't you get another room?"

Utah shook his head. "I don't want to bother anyone. Besides, I think all the available rooms are filled with wedding guests." He could have camped in one of his teammate's rooms, but he didn't have their keys and didn't want to bother the night clerk and have him ask questions.

Liza shook her head. "We can't kick you out of your room. Tayla and I can sleep in your truck."

Utah tipped his chin toward the sleeping three-year-old. "It gets cold outside at night in the Crazy Mountains. I couldn't sleep in my warm bed knowing you two could die of exposure." He gave her a brief smile. "A sofa will be great compared to some places I've had to sleep while on a maneuver." He stepped through the door. "Sleep well. The chef has a special breakfast planned for the guests staying at the lodge. You can join them, or I'll bring a tray for you and Tayla."

Liza clasped her hands together. "You've already done so much for us."

He nodded. "I'll bring a tray. Sleep in. I'll be up and moving around early. I'll come by and check on you around seven if that's not too soon."

"Seven would be fine. I doubt I'll sleep."

"You should be safe here," Utah said. "Even if they have a tracker on that truck, no one knows who picked you up or where you were taken." He pointed to the cap on her head. "The cameras wouldn't have picked up your face beneath the bill of that cap. I think you're good for the night."

Though Liza nodded, Utah could tell she wasn't convinced.

"I'll be close by in case anything happens," he added.

"You'll be in the lobby?" she asked.

He nodded and pointed to his right. "It's at the end of this corridor. You can't get lost. Goodnight, Liza. Maybe tomorrow you can tell me your last name."

As he pulled the door closed, he heard her whisper, "Gray."

Utah stood for a moment with his hand on the doorknob, going over all that had happened since he'd left the bar in Bozeman. Everything centered on one young woman's daring bid for freedom.

Liza Gray.

He listened for sounds of movement inside his room. The door was an original, made of solid wood, an effective sound insulator. After a full minute, Utah released his hold on the knob and stepped back.

With only a few short hours until the vendors arrived, he was strangely reluctant to find that sofa in the lobby to catch some much-needed sleep. He didn't want to leave Liza and Tayla alone.

Which made no sense.

They were safely locked inside. Like he'd said, no one knew he'd brought them there. It wasn't like he'd be very far away in the lobby.

Tucking his sleeping bag under his arm, he forced himself to walk to the end of the hallway, emerging into the lobby with the high ceilings, welcoming furniture and massive stone fireplace. The fire had been tamped down for the night and the next day's festivities.

Murdock and Gabbie had chosen the lodge lobby for the location of the wedding ceremony. The reception would be held in the lodge dining room, where the lodge's chef, Dezi Thomas, would provide the meal with one of her signature culinary masterpieces. Gabbie had left it up to Dezi to "surprise" them.

It didn't matter what Dezi prepared; it would be amazing.

Utah had gained a few pounds since the pretty brunette had started work at the lodge. And he'd never seen Grimm happier. Love had taken the hard edge off his teammate. Not that he was any less effective as a Delta Force operator. He was just more in touch with his feelings where Dezi was concerned.

Utah wondered how that felt. He'd had several relationships over the years. None of them had inspired in him the level of commitment he'd witnessed from the members of his team, who'd found their women since they'd been in Montana.

He tossed his sleeping bag on the couch closest to

the fireplace. Embers still glowed beneath the ash, still providing heat. It would be nice to share the warmth with someone else. How long had it been since he'd been on a date?

Utah shook his head. Too long. Not one woman he'd met since his return from Afghanistan had sparked his interest. None of them could relate to him, his time in the Marine Corps, the years he'd spent in foreign countries, defending his country. Most women, who'd never been in the military or gone to war, were more concerned about what clothes they wore or where they should get their nails done.

In the countries where he'd fought, the people there worried about where they'd get their next meal or where the next bomb would explode. They weren't juggling an office job and taking their kids to baseball practice. They were walking miles to get to fresh water, afraid to let their children run and play for fear of them stepping into a minefield.

Since coming back to the States, Utah had been a little lost. He hadn't felt like he fit in his own country —until Hank Patterson had contacted him, asking if he'd be interested in joining his organization, the Brotherhood Protectors. He'd explained that the men he hired were prior military, like him, men who'd trained as elite special forces—Army Rangers and Delta Force operatives, Navy SEALs, Marine Force

Reconnaissance and members of Air Force Pararescue teams.

They brought their hard-earned experience to the civilian world, providing protection, rescuing kidnap victims and anything else where their skills were needed.

Utah had listened with interest. He'd missed the comradery of the Marine Corps and had been tempted to accept Hank's offer. But when it had come right down to it, he realized he was tired of fighting. He wanted a job where he could see the fruits of his labors. A job where he could build things, not kill.

Hank, a Navy SEAL in his past life, had understood and had known of just the job for him in his hometown. That's how Utah had come to work at the Lucky Lady Lodge, where he'd reunited with men he'd crossed paths with while on active duty. Soldiers and sailors he'd fought alongside, who understood and embraced the comradery that had been missing since they'd left active duty. He'd found his people and hope for a brighter future.

His thoughts went to the woman down the hallway. A brave woman who'd run the gauntlet of gunfire to free herself and her daughter from captivity.

She'd find it difficult to assimilate into society after what she'd been through. And she didn't have the shared experience Utah had lived with his brothers in arms or a Hank Patterson to help her find her way in a world where she no longer belonged.

Utah glanced toward the reception desk. The night clerk had locked the lobby doors after ten and would be in the office behind the desk. If guests needed anything, they had only to ring the bell on the counter to get his attention.

Not wanting to disturb the young man, Utah walked quietly past the front desk to the dining room. Gabbie always left food in the commercial refrigerator for those who wanted to make a late-night snack.

Utah entered the kitchen and opened the refrigerator to find a plastic container filled with slices of ham. His stomach rumbled as he set the container on the counter and rummaged in the crisper for lettuce and tomatoes.

Minutes later, he'd built two huge ham sandwiches with thick slices of homemade bread slathered with mayonnaise and mustard.

He placed them on plates and the plates on a tray. Filled two glasses with ice and poured fresh-squeezed lemonade into them.

Holding the tray with both hands, he carried it through the dining room, the lobby and down the corridor, stopping in front of his room.

He shifted the tray, balancing it on one hand and knocked lightly on the door. If she didn't answer on the first knock, he'd walk away, assuming she was already asleep.

He waited, straining to hear even the slightest noise. Moments passed.

Figuring she'd gone to sleep, Utah turned away with his tray set for two and headed toward the lobby.

He had gone two steps when the click of a lock disengaging brought him to a halt. As he turned back, the door opened.

Liza poked her towel-wrapped head out. "Sorry, I'd just stepped out of the shower when I heard you knock. It took me a moment to find something to wear." Her eyes widened when she spotted the sandwiches.

"I thought you might be hungry," he said.

"We ate before we left the compound, but wow." She licked her lips. "Those look amazing. Is that ham?"

He nodded. "It is."

"Do you want to bring it in here?"

Utah grinned. "Or we could have a picnic in the hall…"

She shook her head. "I'd rather eat at the table in here." Stepping back, she held the door open for him to enter.

Once he cleared the doorway, Liza hurried ahead of him and moved his books and a backpack from the table's surface and pulled two chairs closer.

Utah couldn't help but notice her bare legs beneath an oversized T-shirt that hung past her thighs.

His eyes narrowed. Was it one of his shirts?

"I hope you don't mind. I borrowed one of your shirts. I washed my clothes in the shower and hung them to dry, but they were too wet to put back on." She turned to face him, her cheeks pink.

His groin tightened at the thought of his shirt covering her naked body. "That's fine. Help yourself to whatever you need." He set one of the plates and a glass of lemonade on the surface, then hesitated. It might not be a good idea to stay in the same room with her, especially if he was thinking about her naked body beneath his shirt.

The right thing to do would be to leave her food and beat a hasty retreat to the lobby, where he could eat his sandwich alone. Away from her and her legs.

For a man who usually did the right thing, Utah wasn't operating in his right mind. He hesitated. That was his downfall.

CHAPTER 6

Liza looked at him expectantly. "Aren't you going to stay and eat with me?"

Inside, he warred with his conscience. "Is that what you want?"

Her clean cheeks flushed a deeper pink. "Please. You went to all the trouble, and...well...I kind of got used to having you around."

He chuckled. "Does that mean you trust me?"

Her brow twisted. "I wouldn't go that far. But you haven't tried to hurt Tayla or me."

"There is that." His conscience lost. Utah laid the second plate across from the first and his glass of lemonade beside it. He leaned the tray against the wall and held out one of the seats.

Liza hesitated. "I'll be right back." She turned and ducked into the bathroom, closing the door behind her.

"Too long," he muttered.

"What did you say?" she called out from the other side of the door.

"It's been too long since I've had a good ham sandwich," he replied, willing his rising desire to abate. Otherwise, he'd be highly uncomfortable sitting across the tiny table from the woman stirring his loins.

He turned toward the bed where Tayla lay sleeping.

Bright blond hair spilled across the pillow. Her cheeks had been washed clean, and the comforter had been pulled up to her chin.

Utah couldn't tell if she was breathing. The blanket didn't rise and fall enough to reassure him. A little anxious for proof of life, he leaned closer until he finally registered the barest of movement.

He straightened, releasing the breath he hadn't known he was holding.

The door behind him opened with a creak.

Utah turned as Liza emerged.

She'd removed the towel from her hair and combed the long strands straight, letting them hang down to the middle of her back.

Her lips twisted in a wry grin as she crossed the short distance and slid into the seat he'd held for her earlier, the T-shirt rising up her thigh, exposing more of her smooth skin. "You didn't have to wait. I just didn't want to eat with a towel on my head. I'd have been done before you arrived with the sandwiches, but the hot shower felt too good. I didn't want to get out." She sighed. "It's been a long time since I've had a hot shower. When the water's cold, you don't linger."

Utah could imagine her life over the past ten months. He'd been in places where a shower, even a cold one, was a luxury.

She reached down to her ankle and removed what looked like a small piece of tissue and tossed it into the trashcan beside her with a grimace. "I cut myself shaving. You'd think I'd forgotten how after ten months." She glanced up. "Sorry. I shouldn't be this excited about a shower, but…I am."

He sank into the seat in front of her, thankful the tabletop hid her legs from his gaze. He'd have been fine if he hadn't seen those silky, smooth legs. Now, they were all he could think about.

Utah lifted the sandwich and took a bite, hoping to divert his senses to food, not her.

Liza bit into hers at the same time. As she chewed, her eyes drifted closed, and she moaned. "So good."

He swallowed hard, his thoughts nowhere near food and now focused on her lips and the long line of her throat. "Didn't they feed you at the camp?" he managed to choke out.

She nodded and swallowed. "Mostly stew and soups with potatoes and vegetables. Sometimes, there was meat. When we got sandwiches, it was bologna or peanut butter. If I never see another peanut butter sandwich, I'll be okay with that." She took another bite and moaned again.

Utah swallowed hard on a groan. Eating with this woman was a mistake. He was about to get up when she swallowed, set her sandwich down and lifted her glass. "So, you were a Marine?" She took a sip of the drink, her gaze on him.

"I was."

"And now, you're not." Her brow wrinkled. "Did you retire?"

He shook his head. "I left after ten years."

"Why?"

He stared down at his sandwich, memories washing over him. "I'd had enough. Enough deployments that I couldn't keep track of how many and enough death. Especially of men I considered brothers." He looked up into the bluest eyes he'd ever seen.

"It's hard to lose the people you love," she said softly.

"Yes, it is," he agreed. "You lost your parents."

She nodded. "I was young when my mother died of cancer. It was just me, my brother and my dad for the longest. He was always there for us, and he was there when Tayla was born. I couldn't have done it without him." She stared down at her sandwich. "Tayla was only two when he died of a massive heart attack in his sleep. When he didn't get up for breakfast, I went into his room to wake him up so he wouldn't be late for work." She inhaled and let out a long breath.

Utah waited. It was her story.

She looked up with a sad smile. "He didn't wake up."

"I'm sorry," he said.

"Yeah. Me, too." She stared across the room at the child sleeping peacefully. "Then it was just Tayla and me."

"How were you kidnapped?"

Her gaze shifted to the far corner of the room. "My dad did his best to help us. We lived in Valier, a little town where you could throw a rock from one end to the other. I'd been working part-time at a diner when I got pregnant. I had insurance, but the out-of-pocket expenses with deductibles and co-payments were more than I could afford."

"And Tayla's father didn't help," Utah said.

Liza shook her head. "He left for Seattle as soon as I told him I was pregnant. Nathan accused me of getting pregnant to trap him into marriage. He said if I tried to claim him as the father, I'd have to prove it." Her mouth pressed into a thin line. "He said if I put his name on the birth certificate and came after him for child support, he'd sue for full custody and tell the courts I was an unfit mother."

Utah frowned. "Why would he sue for custody if he didn't want Tayla in the first place?"

Her lips twisted. "He said it to scare me. I knew he

wouldn't sue for custody. But if he did, and there was even the slightest chance he'd win, I'd lose my baby." She shook her head. "I let it go. I would take care of her on my own. His name wasn't on the birth certificate. He has no claim on her.

"I didn't know it, but my father had taken a second mortgage on the house when my mother got cancer. He worked repairing cars. Some people didn't pay him for the work he did. It was all he could do to make both mortgage payments and put food on the table. After Tayla was born, I went back to work part-time but paid more in daycare than I made." She shook her head. "Here I am, rattling on when you only asked how we got kidnapped."

"It's okay," he said. "I'm interested in the full story."

"Bottom line is that when my father died, the bank foreclosed on the house. The diner where I worked let me go because they didn't have enough business to keep me on. I took what little cash my father had in his bank account, packed up what I could fit into his old truck and headed for Bozeman, where I hoped to find work that would help me support my daughter."

"Why Bozeman? Great Falls would've been closer."

She nodded. "Hindsight being twenty-twenty, I should've gone to Great Falls. Instead, I chose Bozeman because Great Falls had too many memories of growing up with my father and brother. Bozeman was where my mother had grown up. I'd always wanted to see the town where she'd been raised and gone to school. She'd turned out pretty great. From how she described it, the town seemed the perfect place to raise Tayla." Liza met Utah's gaze. "I was twenty miles outside of Bozeman when the truck broke down. It was late afternoon, and it had started to snow. I was afraid and desperate to get Tayla somewhere warm." Liza's jaw tightened, and a shadow crossed her eyes.

Utah's gut knotted. He reached across the table and took her hand, holding it gently in his.

"A truck pulled up behind mine. A couple of men got out. I thought they were going to help me. I told them I was heading to Bozeman. When they offered to give us a ride, I accepted."

Her gaze dropped to her hand in his. "I gathered up Tayla and climbed into that truck. It wasn't until we left the highway to Bozeman that I realized we were in trouble."

She looked toward her sleeping daughter. "Tayla turned three in that camp. She didn't have a cake or presents. She's outgrown the clothes and shoes we arrived in. I had no way of providing more for her. I told myself that every day we were still alive and together was a good day. I promised myself that when we were rescued, I'd give her the birthday party she deserved and never let anyone harm her or take her away from me."

As she'd talked, her fingers tightened on his.

"You got out," he said. "That's what matters. You're free of them."

"But for how long? They put a lot of time and effort into training me. They're not going to let me just waltz right out without repercussions."

"Training you for what?" Utah asked.

LIZA WISHED she hadn't said anything about her training. She looked across the table at him, trying to guess what his response would be if she told him what they'd wanted her to do.

His hand tightened slightly around hers. "I'm not going to judge you," he said. "Those people did awful things to you and shouldn't be allowed to get away with it."

She pulled her hand from his. This man had saved her life. Would he regret having done it when he knew the truth?

"Liza, nothing you can tell me will make me feel any differently toward you. You were in an impossible situation just trying to stay alive."

She met his gaze and held it. "They were training me to be an assassin."

His eyes widened for a brief second. Then he was on his feet, heading for the door.

Liza's heart plummeted to the pit of her belly.

The man obviously regretted having anything to do with her and would walk out that door, wishing he'd left her on the side of the road.

Utah didn't walk out the door. He spun and shoved a hand through his hair. "Holy shit," he said quietly. "This camp you were in…what was its name? What did they call it?"

She frowned. "We only knew it as The Camp. Why?"

He crossed to stand in front of her, his gaze intense, his fists clenched. "Did they mention the name of their network?"

She shook her head. "They were very tight-lipped about names, whether it was names of the recruits, trainers or the compound."

"Did they ever mention a group called The Chosen Way?"

"Not that I heard." Liza's eyes narrowed. "What are you thinking?"

"You mentioned that one of the camps was overrun, and some people from there came to your location."

She nodded. "I did overhear some of the new guys mention a TCW." Her eyes widened.

Utah nodded. "The. Chosen. Way."

Now that she knew what the letters stood for, she wasn't that much wiser. "What is The Chosen Way?" she asked.

He smacked his palm against his forehead. "I can't believe I didn't put it together sooner."

"Put what together sooner?" Her head was spinning, and what little she'd eaten of the sandwich churned in her belly. She pushed to her feet. "You're not making sense."

"Kidnapped children and adults...training them as fighters... They're all part of The Chosen Way, an organization created to produce killers. The Camp you were in is just one of their training sites. We busted up one not long ago, west of Anaconda, outside a little town called Last Resort." He gripped her arms. "Could you find your way back to that camp?"

She shook her head. "I'm not going back, even if I could find my way there."

"I don't want you to go back. I want you to lead us there. These people have to be stopped. They're brainwashing children into becoming killers."

Liza nodded. "I know. When they gave me my first assignment, I told them no way." She tilted her chin toward Tayla. "Then they threatened to take Tayla away from me if I didn't go through with it."

Utah's face hardened. "Bastards."

"I knew I had to get out. I couldn't live with myself if I killed someone who didn't deserve to die." She frowned. "I got out, but that doesn't mean my target will be forgotten." She looked up into Utah's eyes. "They'll send someone else to do the job."

"That person must be warned," Utah said. "And the camp needs to be shut down and the people running it sent to jail."

Liza pushed free of his grip, walked to the side of the bed and stared down at her daughter. "I can't go back," she said.

"You only have to show us where it is. We'll take it from there."

She shook her head. "I left so fast I don't think I could find my way back, even if I wanted to."

"We can try to retrace your steps. Work backward through the towns you passed by or through, the highway signs you might remember, the directions you were heading when you saw signs." He turned her around. "You know you can't leave the others there, knowing what's happening to them."

Liza thought of PJ and how she'd helped her to escape. She prayed PJ hadn't been caught aiding her mad dash for freedom. She thought about the others who'd been forced to train, punished for the slightest infractions, and sometimes, beaten to within an inch of their lives.

"The longer we wait, the more time they have to pack up and move to another location," he said softly. "I know people who can move on this ahead of law enforcement. People who can keep your location a secret."

"That group you didn't go to work for?"

He nodded. "The Brotherhood Protectors." He

pulled his cell phone from his back pocket. "I can call the boss, Hank Patterson. He'd know exactly what to do and mobilize his people to make it happen."

She shook her head. "What about Tayla?"

"He can provide her protection as well."

"I can't pay him," Liza said.

"I've heard he doesn't take assignments based on who can pay. If someone needs help, he'll send his people."

She stared into Utah's eyes. "Promise me this isn't all just a bunch of bullshit."

He held up his fingers like a Boy Scout again. "I promise, this isn't just a bunch of bullshit."

"Promise me you're one of the good guys."

He grinned. "I promise. I'm one of the good guys."

She drew in a deep breath and nodded. "Call in the Brotherhood Protectors."

Utah scrolled through his contacts, found what he was looking for and hit the call button. He walked away from Liza and Tayla.

Liza strained to hear the sound of the phone ringing but couldn't.

She didn't have long to wait.

Within seconds, Utah spoke. "Hank, Utah here. Remember the raid we did on The Chosen Way?" He nodded and listened. "I might have someone who knows where another camp is located. This person escaped tonight… Right…they'll be scrambling to get the others moved before the escapee shows the authorities where they are. No, sir…my team isn't available. They're sleeping off a bachelor party in Bozeman. The wedding is…" Utah glanced at his watch, "later today." He turned to face Liza. "Yes, my informant is willing to help locate the compound. Yes, sir. We'll be looking for you after the sun comes up. Thank you, sir." He ended the call, his gaze locked on Liza's.

"What did he say?" Liza asked.

"Hank's on board." Utah shoved his phone into his back pocket. "He'll arrive in a helicopter at sunup. He and his computer guy, Swede, will help you figure out how far you came and from which direction. Once they have a good idea of where to look, they'll go up in the chopper and conduct an aerial reconnaissance of the area."

"If they find them, then what?" she asked.

"He'll have his team heading in that general direction, ready to move in once the compound is located."

Liza's pulse pounded through her veins. She didn't regret her decision to go back for the others. Still, she prayed she wasn't exposing herself and Tayla to the possibility of re-capture or worse… termination.

CHAPTER 7

"For now, you might as well get some sleep," Utah said. "I'll be close by if you need me."

Liza shook her head. "I don't think I could sleep. I'm too wound up."

"Then lay down and let your body recover, even if you don't go to sleep. I'm going to do the same. We can't do much until Hank arrives."

Liza's brows drew together. "You trust Hank?"

He nodded solemnly. "With my life."

"Would you trust him with the lives of someone you love?"

Again, he nodded. "Without a single doubt."

"I'm trusting your word, betting my daughter's life on it," she said.

"If I had a daughter in trouble like Tayla, I'd trust Hank completely."

Her lips twisted. "I guess it doesn't matter. It's a

done deal now. Someone besides you and I knows where I am. It could be only a matter of time before TCW, or whoever they are, finds me." She sighed. "You're right. I need to rest. What happens next might require even more of me than my escape from The Camp."

She walked with him to the door and held it open for him to pass through it. "I hope you get some sleep. You have a wedding to plan. At least by handing me off to Hank, you won't have to feel responsible for us."

Utah took her hand in his. "It's not that simple," he said. "I did save your life. I won't walk away from you just because Hank's taking over. By saving your life…"

She held up her hand. "No. You are not responsible for my life. You have your own to live." Liza tipped her head toward the empty corridor. "Go. Get some sleep so that you can live your life at your best."

He wanted to tell her he would never relinquish that responsibility. Yet, he knew she would argue the issue, using up more of the short time they had left to replenish their energy stores. He cupped her cheek and stared down into her eyes. "Get some rest."

Then he bent and touched his lips to hers in the softest of kisses. As soon as his mouth touched hers, he was shocked at both how natural it felt and how badly timed the gesture was.

This woman had been through so much. Her

captors had abused and tormented her and threatened the only thing that meant anything to her…her child. She sure as hell didn't need her so-called rescuer putting the move on her.

Though he didn't want to stop kissing her, he lifted his head, severing their connection but not putting any more distance between them.

When he'd gone in for the kiss, her hands had come up to rest on his chest. As he lifted his head, those hands rose to encircle the back of his neck, bringing him back to her.

This time when their mouths touched, he was helpless to stop. He pulled her closer until her hips pressed against him and his growing desire nudged her belly.

He swept his tongue across the seam of her lips.

She opened to him, and he plunged in, claiming her in a kiss that rocked him so completely that everything around him faded. All he could see, smell and sense was the woman in his arms.

When he finally raised his head, he realized they were still standing in the open door.

Liza stared up at him, her eyes widening.

Though the kiss had been more like an out-of-body experience to him, it might have felt like more male aggression to Liza.

He stepped back. "I shouldn't have done that."

She shook her head, her hand rising to her kiss-swollen lips. "No, we shouldn't have."

"The gentleman in me ought to say I'm sorry. But maybe I'm not the gentleman I thought I was. I can't say I'm sorry…because I'm not." Utah shoved a hand through his hair. "Oh, hell. Close the door, Liza. Close it before I kiss you again."

When she made no move to do as he'd suggested, he leaned toward her.

She lifted her face to him, and her lips parted ever so softly.

God, he wanted to kiss her again. With every ounce of control he could muster, he reached out, grabbed the doorknob and pulled the door closed between them.

Utah leaned his forehead against the cool wood and muttered a silent curse.

The woman had suffered enough. She didn't need to worry about him mauling her with kisses she'd never asked for.

"Utah?" her muffled voice sounded through the thick wood panel. "Are you still there?"

"Yeah." He pressed his palm to the wood as if he could feel her on the other side.

"I'm not sorry, either," she said so softly he could barely make out her words.

His heart turned a crazy somersault.

"Utah?" she called out again.

"What, Liza?" he answered.

"Thank you."

He frowned, not expecting those words. "For what?"

"For reminding me that I'm just a girl with needs and dreams like any other girl." She paused and added, "Not a killer."

Her last words gutted him.

The people who'd abducted her had tried to change a sweet, passionate young woman into a killer.

Had she gone through with their plan in order to save her daughter, they would have owned her for the rest of her life, or she would've felt compelled to turn herself in for murder. Either way, her life would've been ruined. Furthermore, no court in the land would have allowed her to keep Tayla, even if she got a plea bargain and a light sentence.

After several long minutes of silence, Utah left the door and returned to the lobby. He grabbed his sleeping bag and returned to the hallway outside his door.

Opening the bag, he spread it out in front of the door and lay on top of it. Though it was cool in the hall, he wanted to remain free of entanglements should he have to rise quickly to protect the two girls in his room.

Free of entanglements.

He laughed softly. Those words had been his mantra for his entire adult life. Until now.

That kiss had entanglement written all over it.

Yet, it didn't dampen his desire to do it again. In fact, it fed the flames, making him want to go back for more.

He lay on his back, staring at the ceiling, knowing he wouldn't sleep. Not with his thoughts roiling around in his head.

When he'd left the pub and his friends several hours earlier, he'd had a clear vision of his future, working as a handyman, restoring buildings and spending time with his buddies. Never in those scenarios had he envisioned ending the night kissing a would-be assassin and offering to protect said assassin and her three-year-old daughter. He didn't even like kids.

An image of Tayla standing near the edge of a horrible drop-off, her little body shivering in the night air made him think, for a child, she might not be so bad. She'd stuck up for him and believed him when he'd said he was one of the good guys. Her mother hadn't been convinced. And after he'd come onto Liza so strong, she might not be convinced he was a good guy and think she should stay as far away from him as possible.

Sometime after two o'clock, Utah must have drifted off. He woke with a start when the door he lay in front of opened slowly, and Liza's face appeared in the gap.

He sat up instantly. "Everything okay?"

Her lips twisted. "Sorry. I didn't mean to wake

you. I feel bad that you're sleeping out here when we're in a soft, warm bed. At the very least, you should have this." She opened the door wider and handed him a pillow.

He smiled. "Thanks. You should be asleep."

She nodded. "I dozed. But I felt bad about you being out here after all you've done for us. And whenever you want it, you can have your gun back."

He tucked the pillow behind his head and lay back with a smile. "Keep it for now," he said. "I feel better knowing you have some protection if I don't happen to be around.

She dipped her head. "Thank you." Closing the door slowly, she whispered, "Good night, Utah."

"Good night, Liza."

She closed the door between them.

Silence reigned except for the deafening beat of Utah's pulse pounding against his eardrums. The woman had an alarming effect on him, and that just wouldn't do.

He laced his fingers behind his head and settled back against the sleeping bag and the soft, fluffy pillow.

The woman who'd held a gun on him for most of their time together had offered him a pillow and felt guilty for taking his bed.

He chuckled. And they'd trained her to be an assassin? He frowned. She didn't have it in her to kill someone.

Then he pictured the angelic three-year-old and Liza's fierce protective instinct where her daughter was concerned.

Her captors had zeroed in on the only thing that would motivate Liza to even consider killing another person.

Tayla.

And yet, she'd risked her life, stolen a truck and braved live gunfire to get herself and her daughter out of an impossible situation.

He didn't blame her for wanting to keep running. If TCW's network was as widespread as Liza thought, she might never be safe. He hoped that shutting down the compound where she'd trained and capturing those who'd held her hostage would be enough or a good start in eradicating the criminals stealing people from their homes and lives and turning them into killing machines.

Over the next two hours, he dozed off and on. At four-thirty, he got up, rolled up his sleeping bag, grabbed the pillow and stashed them in a supply closet a few doors down. He wandered out into the lobby, watching for the delivery trucks that would be arriving soon.

He met Dezi Thomas as she entered through the front door, using the key card she'd been entrusted with when she'd signed on as the head chef of the Lucky Lady Lodge.

Despite the shadows beneath her eyes and her

makeup-free face, she smiled brightly. "Good morning," she called out. "Are we ready for Murdock and Gabbie's big day?"

Utah shrugged, not as chirpy in the morning as the ever-cheerful Dezi. "We will be. The question is, are the bride and groom ready? It's a big step."

Dezi's grin broadened. "Oh, they're ready. Gabbie couldn't wait to call it a night, insisting she get some sleep. She didn't want to look like death when she showed up for the ceremony."

"Did she get that sleep?"

Dezi laughed. "Though she told everyone she wouldn't take any emergency calls last night, she disappeared around one o'clock in the morning to help a rancher's prize mare deliver a breech foal." The perky chef shook her head. "We didn't even know she was gone until I passed her coming in as I was leaving her place thirty minutes ago."

"Did everything turn out okay for the mare and foal?"

Dezi nodded. "It did. The rancher even said he'd name the foal after Gabbie and Murdock in honor of their wedding day." She leveled a look at him. "Are you just getting in? I thought you weren't going to stay the night in Bozeman like the other guys."

"No. I got in around two after helping the guys get our groom back to the hotel." He wasn't ready to go into all that had happened on his way back from Bozeman. He'd wait to get Hank's take on the situation and the secrecy Liza was so adamant about.

"Then you didn't get much more sleep than I did. I volunteered to sleep in the lounge chair at Gabbie's place. They're going to need a lot bigger one to fit Murdock's big frame." She rolled her shoulders. "Needless to say, I was awake well before my alarm with a thousand thoughts going through my head. I wanted to get here and make a good start at the day's menu before my assistants arrive at six. Thankfully, the cake is ready. After a quick breakfast for the wedding guests, I can focus on the menu for the reception. I want everything to be special."

"Don't let me keep you," Utah said. "I'll look forward to everything you'll make."

"Thanks," she said with a smile. "I'll have coffee ready in ten minutes." With that parting comment, she hurried toward the dining room.

When Utah turned toward the front entrance, he spotted a delivery van pulling in. He hurried to unlock the door for the men delivering the chairs for the ceremony and the arbor the florist would load with flowers.

After all the chairs were set up in front of the massive fireplace and the metal arbor erected, they carried in the linens that would be used in the dining room for the reception.

Utah worked alongside the party rental people to get the job done quickly, his gaze going to the windows in anticipation of the sunrise and Hank's appearance.

The florists arrived as the night faded into the gray light of pre-dawn. He showed them where Gabbie had indicated she'd wanted the flowers placed and left them to their work. Everything was falling into place.

If all went well, Utah hoped to fly with Hank's team in the helicopter to help look for the camp where Liza had been held captive for ten months. He'd like to be the one to get his hands on her trainer, Spike, and Commander, the man in charge of the operation.

With the party planners and the florists busy, he hurried into the kitchen.

"There you are," Dezi sang out. "Pour yourself a cup of coffee and grab a fork. I made an omelet for you." She was busy stirring a skillet full of fluffy scrambled eggs.

"Do you have a tray I could use? I'd like to eat in my room. And do you mind making another omelet?"

Her brow wrinkled. "The omelet is in the warmer. It should be good."

"Thanks, but I'd like another plate." He looked over her shoulder at the eggs in the pan. "And if you don't mind, another plate with some of the scrambled eggs. Is there bacon or sausage?" he asked, looking around.

Dezi laughed as she sprinkled little cubes of ham and tomatoes, bell pepper and chopped green onions into another skillet with a thin layer of olive oil. "Hungry this morning?"

"Something like that," he answered. Using tongs, he added more ham to the skillet, along with bacon bits.

Dezi poured eggs over the meat and vegetables and set the skillet over a flame. While the omelet cooked, she scraped most of the eggs out of the other skillet into a large bowl and filled a plate with what was left.

With quiet efficiency, Dezi pulled out a serving tray, loaded the omelet from the warmer, the scrambled eggs, a plate stacked with pancakes, a small pitcher of syrup and another plate filled with bacon and sausage links.

Utah grabbed juice glasses and filled two with fresh-squeezed orange juice from the refrigerator and one with milk. He set them between the plates, leaving room for the last omelet, which Dezi expertly flipped in half, adding a layer of shredded cheddar cheese across the top before she slid it onto a plate and filled the space on the loaded tray.

"Don't forget the coffee," she reminded him and turned to pull biscuits from the oven.

Utah filled two mugs with freshly brewed coffee and squeezed them onto the tray. Then he lifted it in two arms. "Jesus. How do the wait staff carry these trays on one hand?"

Dezi chuckled. "They get good at balancing over time. I'd hold on with both hands for now."

He carried the tray out of the kitchen, through the dining room, across the lobby and down the hallway to stop in front of his room.

He kicked the door softly with the toe of his boot. "Hey, it's me," he called out.

He waited for what felt like a very long moment. The door remained closed. The pretty blonde who'd taken over his room and his life the night before didn't open it to stick her head out.

He frowned, his gut clenching.

Had she gotten cold feet and snuck out while he'd been busy with the deliveries?

He kicked the door again, some of his desperation adding force to the tip of his boot.

The door opened immediately. Liza looked out, a frown pulling her eyebrows down low. "What's wrong?" Then she spotted the loaded tray, a smile spreading across her face. "Holy smokes, that's enough to feed an army." Her gaze met his, her eyes going wide. "Is that for us?"

He nodded. "If you open the door and let me set it down before I drop it all."

Liza stepped back and held the door wide. She'd changed out of his T-shirt and into the clothes she'd worn when he'd found her. Her hair had been gathered up onto the top of her head in some kind of messy bun. Loose golden strands framed her clean, fresh face. She was beautiful.

"Wow. Oh, wow." Her voice choked. She sat on the edge of the bed and clasped her cheeks in her hands. "I can't believe this is happening. Is this even real?"

Tayla sat up in bed and placed a hand on her mother's back. "It's okay," the little girl said. "It's real. The pancakes look so good, and I can smell them from here."

Liza reached over her shoulder to cup her daughter's face. "I love you, baby."

The little girl wrapped her arms around Liza's neck. "I love you, too, Mommy." She leaned back and glanced at the tray Utah had lowered to the little table. "Are you going to eat with us, Mr. Utah?"

Utah grinned at how Tayla addressed him. For a three-year-old, she spoke like an adult, much like Utah probably had at her age. "It's up to your mother."

Liza nodded. "Of course. Please, eat with us."

The table only had two straight-back chairs. Utah held one of the chairs for Tayla as she scrambled up into it.

When Liza hesitated over the other, he smiled. "Sit and start eating. The sun will be up soon." He met her gaze. Hank would be there soon.

She nodded. "I understand. But where will you sit?"

He tipped his head toward the armchair against the wall.

Liza sank into the chair he held for her. "Thank you."

Once Liza was seated, Utah moved the armchair from the corner up to the table and sat forward on the edge of the cushion so that he could reach the table.

"I wasn't sure what you'd want," he said. "You have your choice of pancakes, an omelet or scrambled eggs, and bacon or sausage."

"My mouth is watering," she said. "It all looks and smells so good."

"Dezi is a great chef," Utah said. "She even makes simple eggs taste gourmet."

"What do you want to eat?" Liza asked.

He smiled. "I like everything. You and Tayla are the guests. You get to choose first."

Liza placed the scrambled eggs in front of Tayla, added a pancake, a strip of crispy bacon and a sausage link.

Tayla waited, her eyes wide, her little tongue sweeping over her lips.

When Utah lifted his fork, the little girl lifted hers. It wasn't until Utah took his first bit of omelet that she dug into her scrambled eggs. She quickly ate half the huge plate of eggs, the entire pancake, the bacon and the sausage link.

Liza scarfed down her omelet before Utah had made it two-thirds through his own.

"Did they feed you breakfast at the camp?" he asked softly.

Liza stared at the slice of bacon in her hand. "Not like this. Sometimes, we got warm oatmeal. Most often, we ate bologna or peanut butter sandwiches."

He chuckled. "And if you never see another peanut butter sandwich…" His smile faded. "I get it."

Liza polished off her slice of bacon and one fluffy pancake. After she washed all of it down with a glass of orange juice, she sat back. "Wow."

Tayla sat back against her seat, her hand on her belly. "My tummy is full."

Liza smiled at her daughter. "Mine, too." She turned to Utah. "Thank you."

"Don't thank me. Thank Dezi. She made this possible."

Liza frowned. "What does she know?"

"About you? Nothing." He laid down his fork and lifted his coffee mug. "I told her I wanted the extra food for one of the guests. She was busy preparing a breakfast buffet for the other wedding guests who will be rising soon. She didn't ask any questions."

Liza nodded. "Any word from your friend Hank?"

"Nothing. He should be here at daylight." Utah

glanced toward the bathroom. "If you don't mind, I want to shower before he gets here. I'd like to tag along on the helicopter if they can get me back by noon." He grimaced. "I'm one of the groomsmen, and the photographer wants us dressed and assembled by one o'clock for pre-wedding photos."

Liza shook her head. "Of course. This is your room. Do what you need to." She rose with her cup of coffee in her hand. "I'm sorry our presence is interfering with your plans."

"Don't be." Utah crossed to the dresser and opened the drawer with his T-shirts and underwear. "You accomplished a great feat, getting out of that place. Don't worry about me. If I don't make it on time, the guys will understand." He selected a black T-shirt and boxer briefs, closed the drawer and reached into the closet for a pair of jeans. "I'll only be a few minutes."

She nodded and took a sip of her coffee, her gaze on him as he turned toward the bathroom.

Utah was relieved she hadn't decided to make a run for it while he'd been working that morning to set up the wedding venue.

The more he was around her, the more he wanted to know about the stranger he'd found on the side of the highway.

He pulled his T-shirt over his head and tossed it into the clothes basket in the corner where the T-shirt she'd worn lay. An image of Liza wearing that T-shirt raised the heat level in the bathroom and made Utah's groin tighten. Glad of the door between them, he shucked his boots and jeans, stepped into the shower and turned on the cold water.

Thinking about Liza in that T-shirt only led him to physical frustration. He'd needed to focus on something that would tamp down the desire making his cock hard.

What about the men she'd had to deal with at the camp? What had she called them? Spike and Commander?

Utah stood beneath the cool spray, allowing the water to run down his front, chill water shrinking his hard shaft effectively. He scrubbed his face and body, rinsed and turned off the shower.

After drying, he slipped into his boxer briefs and jeans, imagining Liza standing on the other side of the door, drinking coffee and talking to Tayla.

What about Tayla?

Utah wasn't usually comfortable around children. But he didn't feel *un*comfortable with Tayla. She spoke to him as if she was an equal, not like most three-year-olds he'd been around. And that hadn't been many. Thankfully, she wasn't a screaming, burping, pooping baby. Those squirming creatures positively scared him.

For a kid, Tayla was all right. And she was the

mini-version of her beautiful mother. The love shared between the two was obvious and profound.

Liza would do anything for that little girl.

Utah hoped she didn't have to kill for her.

CHAPTER 8

Liza combed through Tayla's hair, easing out the tangles. When she was done, she pulled her daughter's hair back to the nape of her neck and was twisting an elastic band around it when her daughter turned her head sharply and stepped away.

"No, Mommy." She reached back to pull the loose band out of her hair. Then she pointed at Liza's hair piled on top of her head. "Like yours. Please."

Liza nodded. "Okay." Tayla hadn't been allowed to wear her hair any other way than in the single braid down the back of her neck.

Liza pulled the wispy strands of baby hair up and secured them at the top of her daughter's head in a messy bun just like her own. She lifted Tayla and carried her to the mirror over the dresser. "So pretty," she said.

Tayla smiled at their reflections in the glass. "Just like you, Mommy."

Liza's heart swelled. "Thank you, sweetie." She set the little girl on the floor and moved to the window. Standing out of view from the ground below, she stared out at the parking lot and the mountains in the distance.

The view was beautiful and tranquil. If she wasn't on the run, it might have been a perfect place to raise a family. She frowned, wishing things could be different.

"What's wrong?" Utah's deep voice sounded behind her.

She jumped and turned to face him, raising a hand to her chest where her heart beat like a snare drum at a rock concert. "Jeez. You startled me."

"Sorry."

"It's okay," she said with a half-laugh. "I'm definitely punchy."

"Understandable." He raised his muscular arms and swept a comb through his wet hair.

Liza's breath caught in her throat. The man was entirely too good-looking for her own good. She swallowed hard and told herself to get a grip. Yet, she couldn't turn away. "That was a fast shower."

"I learned to make it quick when I was deployed to the desert. We didn't get a shower often and had to make do with whatever we could get. Cold, short and once a week, if we were lucky."

"Sounds like The Camp." Her brows knit, and she tipped her head to the side. "Those in charge of us called us 'recruits' and barked at us like they were drill sergeants. It made me wonder if they'd been in the military."

Utah's lips pressed together. "If I knew their real names, I could find out."

The sound of rotors drew Utah to the window. He pulled the black-out curtains open slightly and peered out.

A helicopter lowered slowly onto the overflow parking lot below the lodge.

Utah let the curtain fall in place and turned to Liza. "Hank's here. I'll go see how he wants to handle this and come get you when I know."

Her gaze held his for a long moment.

"Don't worry. If there's anyone you can trust, it's Hank Patterson. He understands the importance of family even better than I do. He has two small children of his own."

Liza nodded slowly. "I'll do anything to protect my daughter. If I have to disappear, I will."

"Understood," Utah said. "I hope you'll give us a chance to prove to you that we're here to help, not hurt you or Tayla." He smiled at the little girl as she sat on the edge of the bed.

She slid off the bed, ran to him, wrapped her arms around his leg and looked up at him with her sky-blue eyes so much like her mother's. "You wouldn't hurt me or Mommy. You're a good guy."

He patted her head, unused to little people holding onto his leg. "That's right."

She let go of his leg and raised her arms.

Utah looked from the little girl to her mother.

Liza's lips quirked. "That means she wants you to pick her up."

He'd held her before, but she'd been asleep. This animated creature was totally different.

He bent and picked her up beneath her arms.

Like an octopus, her arms wrapped around his neck and her legs around his chest. She squeezed hard with her skinny limbs. "You won't leave us, will you?" she whispered in his ear.

Utah looked over the little girl's shoulder to her mother.

Liza's brow puckered. "Sweetie, he has to go do stuff."

"That's right. But I'll be back."

She squeezed harder. "Promise?"

He held her away so that he could look into her eyes. "I promise."

Tayla nodded as if satisfied with his answer. "Okay. You can put me down."

The grown-up way she spoke seemed incongruous with her little voice and features. She was as light as a feather. The word that came to Utah's mind was *fragile*.

How had this little girl survived being in that camp for ten months?

On impulse, he hugged her gently before he set her on her feet. "I'll be back in a few minutes." As he passed Liza, he whispered, "Trust me."

Liza's lips pressed together, but she nodded.

She hadn't run yet, but Utah knew how difficult it must be to place her faith in anyone after where she'd been and what she and her daughter had survived.

He left the room, closing the door behind him. He could hear the metal click of the lock being turned and felt better knowing she wasn't waiting for him to leave before disappearing again.

Utah left the lodge through the side door, crossed the parking lot and met Hank as he headed toward the lodge's main entrance.

When he spotted Utah, he hurried toward him and held out his hand. As Utah shook it, he glanced over his shoulder. "Where is she?"

"In my room. She's afraid to come out or be seen by anyone."

Hank nodded.

A tall man with white-blond hair and broad shoulders joined him, carrying a laptop.

Hank turned to him. "This is my computer guru. Former Navy SEAL, implicitly trustworthy. Swede, this is Pierce Turner."

Utah held out his hand. "Call me Utah."

"Axel Svenson." The guy who looked like a Viking grinned as he introduced himself. "Call me Swede."

Hank glanced up at the building in front of him. "I believe there's a conference room in the lodge with an internet connection. Could we meet with the woman there?"

Utah nodded. It would be easier than cramming three big guys in his small room with Liza and Tayla. "I'll get her and meet you there."

While Hank and Swede continued toward the main entrance, Utah aimed for the side.

He'd barely reached his door when it opened, and Liza waved him inside.

He stepped through the door.

Liza closed it and twisted the deadbolt before facing him.

"Hank wants to meet in the conference room," Utah said. "Are you okay with that?"

Liza's brow furrowed. "There were two men out there. Which one was Hank, and who was the other guy?"

"The blond one was Axel Svenson, Hank's computer guy," Utah said. "He'll help narrow the search to find the compound."

"That's three people who will know where I am. Four, if you count the helicopter pilot." She drew in a deep breath and let it out slowly. "The more people who know, the greater the chance something will get out."

"I know," Utah touched her arm. "I also know we need their help to find the compound. And soon. We can't let them get away. The other captives and that congresswoman are at risk. If Hank's computer guy can help narrow the search, we can get there faster."

Liza reached behind her, pulled the baseball cap out of the back of her waistband and pulled it over her messy bun and down low on her forehead. She crossed to Tayla and fit a beanie cap over the child's head. "I found the cap in one of your bags. I doubt that covering her hair will help disguise us, but if anyone sees her, they might think she's a boy, not a little girl."

"Anything is better than nothing."

"It might buy me a little time." She took Tayla's hand. "We're ready."

Utah opened the door and peered out into the hallway. It was empty. "Clear." He reached for Liza's other hand automatically.

When she placed her hand in his, he was mildly surprised but didn't make a big deal about it. Pleased that she was beginning to trust him, he prayed he was doing the right thing by encouraging her to return to the very place she'd escaped.

He took the long way around to the conference room, checking to make sure the hallways were clear of people before he rounded corners and brought Liza and Tayla with him. Only once did he see someone in a corridor. One of the wedding guests left his room, heading for the dining room.

Utah waited until the man disappeared around a corner before he moved with his entourage.

They made it to the conference room without running into anyone. Once all three of them entered the room, he closed and locked the door behind them.

Hank and Swede sat at the conference table, looking up at a large screen mounted on the wall. Swede had his laptop open, his fingers moving over the keys. A map appeared on the screen. Swede clicked more keys, and the map zoomed in on an area with names of towns, including Bozeman and Eagle Rock.

Hank rose and crossed to where Utah, Liza and Tayla stood. He gave Liza a gentle smile. "Hi. I'm Hank Patterson." He held out his hand.

Liza placed hers in his, her eyes narrowing. She hesitated, looked to Utah and then spoke softly, "I'm Liza Gray."

Utah could only imagine how hard it was for her to tell Hank her name. After ten months of being "Fly" and threatened with severe punishment if she spoke her real name aloud, sharing her name with anyone had to be torture.

"Nice to meet you, Liza. If you'll come over here, we want to try and backtrack through the route you took and maybe narrow down our search area before we go up in the helicopter. Montana is a big state. We can't cover all of it in the short amount of time we have."

He led the way to the table and held out a chair for her to sit beside Swede.

She hesitated.

Hank grinned. "Liza, this is Swede. He's really good at anything related to computers and finding things. He's big and scary looking, but he won't hurt you."

Swede grinned. "Hey, Liza."

Liza answered with, "Hey."

A little hand slipped into Utah's. He glanced down at Tayla. Her gaze was on her mother, her brow puckered.

Utah bent to whisper, "It's okay. These guys are good guys, too."

She looked up at him, searching his eyes for the truth.

He met her gaze with a serious one of his own.

Finally, she turned back to her mother.

Utah led her to a seat across the table from Liza and Swede and helped her up into a padded leather conference chair.

Liza told Hank and Swede about the camp, the locations of the buildings and why she'd escaped.

Hank's eyes widened when she mentioned the target she'd been assigned. "Wyoming Congresswoman Liliana Lightfeather?"

Liza nodded. "That's the one."

Hank's lips curved upward. "We know her. I have a team of protectors who operate out of West Yellowstone. One of my guys is engaged to the congresswoman." He turned to Swede.

"I'm on it," Swede said, his fingers flying over the keyboard.

"We'll get word to the congresswoman that there might be an attempt on her life. Our man in the Yellowstone division will stay close and protect her. Now, let's find that compound."

She stared up at the map, shaking her head. "I don't know where I was; I just wanted to get as far away from there as possible."

Over the next twenty minutes, Swede and Hank questioned Liza. She detailed her escape from the camp and described her route as best she could remember.

Slowly, she was able to name a few of the towns she'd seen listed on road signs or signs announcing the towns as she'd entered.

Liza remembered the time on the clock in the bunkhouse as she'd left with the woman who'd helped her escape.

Utah offered the time he'd found the bullet-ridden truck on the side of the road.

With all the information they collected, Swede traced her trajectory back to somewhere west of a little town called White Rock, situated southwest of Bozeman.

Swede closed his computer. "I've sent the GPS location of White Rock to my cell phone."

Hank helped Liza to her feet. "Ready to go up?"

She shot a glance toward Utah.

"How long will it take to get there, and would I be able to get back by noon?" He hated that he was a member of the wedding party, but he'd promised to stand with the man as a groomsman.

"It will take less time in the air than it took Liza driving," Hank said. "I figure an hour, tops. Give us a couple of hours searching and an hour back…" He glanced at his watch. "We should be able to make it."

Utah pushed to his feet, frowning. "I could let Murdock know I might be late. Or it might be best if I don't go at all."

Liza shook her head. "I'm not going without you."

"Or me." Tayla slipped out of her chair and slid her hand into Utah's.

Liza gave her daughter a reassuring smile. "I'm not going anywhere without you, Tay."

"Or Mr. Utah," the little girl insisted.

Her little hand in his had a bigger effect on Utah than he could have ever imagined. His heart swelled in his chest.

Hank headed for the door. "Call whomever you need in the wedding party. We'll do our best to get you back in time, but I can't promise anything. Our time in the air will also be limited by fuel consumption. We might have to head back sooner if we get low on fuel."

Utah nodded and met Liza's gaze. Liza and Tayla's lives were a higher priority than standing with his friend at his wedding. Murdock would understand. "I'm coming."

"Good," she said softly.

Hank and Swede headed for the door.

Utah and Tayla joined Liza and stood back as Hank unlocked the door. "We'll go out the side door and meet you at the chopper."

Hank nodded. He and Swede left the conference room.

Utah reached for Liza's hand. "Are you sure about this?"

She shook her head. "Not really."

"We don't have to do it."

Again, she nodded. "Yes, we do. I can't stop thinking about PJ and the others. Not to mention Congresswoman Lightfeather. Plus, how many others have they targeted?" She squeezed his hand. "Let's go."

Utah lifted Tayla up in his arms. She wrapped one of her thin little arms around his neck, leaned close and kissed his cheek. Once again, such a little gesture from a miniature person left a big mark on Utah. He met Liza's gaze.

She smiled. "You're one of the good guys."

God, he hoped he was. These two women were counting on him to keep them safe. Leading them back to the place they'd been held captive didn't seem like the best way to keep them safe.

It was Liza's choice. She couldn't leave the others to their fate. Utah would be with her all the way.

Taking the more circuitous route, he led the girls to the side exit, across the parking lot and down to the waiting helicopter.

Hank helped Liza up into a seat and buckled the safety harness. He handed her a headset and plugged it into a port.

Utah climbed in with Tayla and settled the little girl between Liza and himself, doing his best to tighten the harness around her little body. She was too small for the straps. He did his best and fit a headset over her ears.

Then he buckled his harness and slipped a headset over his ears. After he was settled and connected to the communications, he kept a hand on the three-year-old as the helicopter rose from the ground.

Tayla reached for her mother's hand, then his, and held onto a couple of his fingers so tightly he was sure no blood was making it into them. Somehow, he didn't care. She could hang on as long as she needed him. He felt honored that she trusted him after the most recent men in her life had been bad.

The flight to White Rock took less than an hour.

The pilot slowed as he followed the narrow road leading west of the little town.

Liza pressed her forehead against the window and peered out. Utah did the same, searching for straight lines among gaps in tree branches.

The chopper pilot searched in a grid south of the road. At one point, Hank thought he spotted a building in the trees.

The pilot swooped closer. It was a building. An older house with a barn nearby, not the long bunkhouse Liza had described or the mess hall and other outbuildings. With no chain-link fence or concertina wire in sight, the pilot took the helicopter back up and continued his search along the established grid.

The longer they searched the more Liza's shoulders slumped. Utah had begun to doubt they'd find the camp.

"We've got enough fuel for ten more minutes," the pilot said. "Then we'll have to head back."

Utah glanced across at Liza. She sat up straighter, redoubling her effort to find the place that had been so much a part of her nightmare existence for the last ten months. He wanted to reassure her, but only finding the compound would do that. He turned and glanced back at the terrain below the helicopter.

Trees, hills and more trees.

Then in a small clearing, Utah saw a straight line at the edge of a stand of trees. He followed the line into the shadows of the trees. That line continued out the other end of a group of evergreens.

He tensed and searched the shadows surrounding that clearing and spotted more straight lines. "Hey," he said excitedly, "circle back to the left and get closer to that clearing."

The pilot followed Utah's directions and hovered over the clearing.

Liza pressed her face and hands to the window. "That's the bunkhouse," she cried into her mic. "And the mess hall. Over there is the motor pool. This is it. It's the compound. Watch out. They have grenade launchers and missile launchers stored in one of those smaller buildings."

The pilot took the helicopter up and out of range.

Hank had a pair of binoculars pressed to his face, studying the compound. "I don't see any people."

Liza tapped Hank on the shoulder and held out her hand. "Let me look."

He handed her the binoculars.

Liza studied the clearing for a long moment. Finally, she shook her head. "All the vehicles are gone from the motor pool. Follow the dirt road to the paved highway," she directed, aiming the binoculars at the ground below.

The pilot followed the path through the trees to the road.

"They didn't put the gate back. The guards are gone. No one's keeping anyone in or out." She lowered the binoculars and stared across at Utah. "They're all gone." She turned toward the pilot. "Put us down in the clearing. Do it. Now."

"Would they have mined the clearing?" Hank asked.

"It was hard-packed dirt. You'll know if they disturbed it," she said. "Dear, sweet Jesus. I hope they didn't kill all the recruits before they left. Put us down. Oh, please."

The chopper pilot descended into the clearing. Utah watched through the window, searching for any movement in the shadows. Behind one of the buildings was a scorched area where something had burned.

"The burned area has to be where PJ blew up the propane tank," Liza said. "It burned the side of the mess hall." She shook her head, her body shaking.

Once they touched the ground, Liza fought with the buckles holding her hostage in the harness.

Utah hurried to release his. To Tayla, he said. "Stay here."

She grabbed his hand. "Don't leave me."

"We'll be right back."

"No. Please. Don't leave me."

"Someone needs to stay with the pilot. It's a big job only a big girl can do," Liza said, still struggling with a buckle. "We aren't leaving you. We're going to look around. We'll be right back." She managed to release the last buckle and flung open the side door.

"I promise," Utah said, removing his headset. "I'll be right back."

Tayla didn't look convinced but stayed where she was, still strapped into the harness.

Utah shoved open his door and dove out, ducking low beneath the spinning rotors.

He raced around to the other side of the aircraft to where Liza stood, clear of the blades.

A frown creased her forehead as she turned all around. "They're gone."

CHAPTER 9

Liza couldn't believe what she was seeing, or rather, what she wasn't seeing. Every vehicle that had been parked near the motor pool, even the ones she'd stabbed the front tires on, were gone. The big school bus with the blacked-out windows was gone, the trailer with the generator, the one with the water tank, the other with the fuel tank…all gone.

She ran toward the bunkhouse, a giant hand squeezing her chest, making it hard for her to breathe. The door was closed. When she turned the handle, she didn't expect it to open.

It did.

Terrified of what she might find inside, she opened the door slowly.

Utah appeared beside her as she stared into the shadowy interior, her breath lodged in her throat.

Beside her, Utah held up his cell phone, the flashlight on it engaged, shining into the interior.

It was empty. Down to the wooden floor. The metal bunks were gone. The old wooden footlockers that had been positioned at the ends of each bunk were gone.

The recruits were gone.

Liza let go of the breath she'd held and sagged to her knees. "Thank God," she said. "They took the recruits. I was so afraid they wouldn't. That they'd…" She shook her head. "As long as they're alive…" Liza looked up at Utah, "there's hope."

Utah held out his hand.

Liza placed hers in his and let him draw her to her feet.

They left the bunkhouse and found Hank coming from the mess hall.

"Every building is empty. They cleaned it out," he said. "They didn't leave behind so much as a paperclip. Come on," Hank said. "We need to head back. I'll have someone come out and dust for prints. Though I'm betting they even cleaned those off."

Liza looked around the clearing where she'd stood the day before and thrown a knife at Tayla. The hay bales were gone. She bent to touch a few straws that had been missed. When she straightened, she shivered.

"Ten months, this place was our prison," she whispered. "Now, it seems so…innocuous. There's no one yelling, no one being punched in the gut. No one threatening to kill you."

"It's just a place," Utah said.

Liza nodded. "A place I don't ever want to come back to." She headed for the helicopter and her reason for living. Tayla.

Tayla sat where she'd left her, silent tears slipping from the corners of her eyes.

Liza slid onto the seat beside her and hugged her around the straps holding her. "Told you we wouldn't leave you."

Utah climbed in beside her and held out his hand.

Tayla wrapped her fingers around his and brought his hand into the hug Liza was giving her.

"Mommy," she said. "Can we go now?"

Liza nodded. "Yes, baby." She buckled her harness and held Tayla's hand as the helicopter rose above the compound.

She didn't look down, didn't look back. Her life had been on hold while she'd been a captive in The Camp. Now, it lay ahead of her.

She'd make it a good one for her and Tayla. If she had to leave Montana and go as far away as she could, she would.

She stared over the top of Tayla's head at the man who'd rescued her from the side of the road and realized he'd been right when he'd said he was one of the good guys. Liza wasn't sure what would have happened to her and Tayla if he hadn't come along when he had.

But she couldn't let herself rely on him. If the TCW tracked her down, she and Tayla had to be prepared to run and leave everything and everyone behind.

But for today, she felt somewhat safe with this man and his friend Hank. She just hoped she wasn't putting her and Tayla's life in danger by letting down her guard.

The flight back didn't take long at all, getting them there well before noon.

There were a few more cars in the parking lot.

Though Utah tried to get Liza and Tayla up to the lodge quickly, they weren't fast enough. Once they'd cleared the rotors and started moving up the rise to the main parking area, the chopper rose behind them with the pilot and Hank.

A black SUV pulled in front of the main entrance. Several men piled out, laughing and joking. One of them spotted the trio on the edge of the lot.

"Hey, Utah!" One of them shouted, waving at the departing helicopter. "What the hell?"

Utah glanced down at Liza. "I'm sorry we're not going to make it into the lodge undetected."

Liza pulled the hat down lower on her forehead. "It's okay. Arriving back at the lodge in a helicopter was bound to draw attention." She tipped her head toward the men. "I take it one of those guys is the groom."

Utah nodded. "The tallest one with black hair and blue eyes. Or rather bloodshot eyes." He chuckled. "I bet he's got one helluva a hangover. Come on." He lifted Tayla up in his arms and crossed to where his buddies were unloading garment bags and shoe boxes from the back of the vehicle.

"Dude," a man with short, sandy-blond hair clapped a hand on Utah's back. "I thought you were here helping them set up for the wedding. What's with the helicopter?"

Utah shook his head. "It's a long story."

"Who've you got with you?" the man asked, chucking Tayla beneath the chin before his gaze fell on Liza with her cap pulled low.

"Molly and Parker said we could all get ready in the conference room," Utah said. "How about we go there, and then I'll tell you what I've been up to."

"You might as well bring the kid and your friend with you. My amazing little chef is serving us lunch there." He grinned at Liza and Tayla. "I can't wait to hear what you were doing in a helo." He looped a garment bag over his shoulder, tucked a shoe box under his arm and followed the groom and other groomsmen into the building.

"Do you want to take the long way?" Utah asked Liza.

She shook her head. "Let's just blend in with the others. All eyes will be on the groom."

They hurried to catch up and blend in with the others as they entered the lodge and made their way to the conference room.

Once inside, the guys hung their garment bags on a coat rack and gathered around the conference table.

While Utah, Tayla and Liza had been gone, someone had transformed the table into a buffet filled with food. Hearty sandwiches were stacked at one end. A full range of cheese and crackers were artfully layered at the other, with an entire assortment of fresh fruit beside it.

The door to the conference room opened, and a man and an auburn-haired woman entered carrying an ice chest between them.

"We brought the beer and sodas," the man called out.

Utah whispered to Liza, "That's Molly and Parker. They own the lodge. They hired us to help with the remodel."

A moment later, the couple was followed by a petite brunette as she backed in, carrying a massive tray of assorted sliders. When she turned around, she grinned. "Oh, good. You're all here. I was afraid we'd have to send out a search party to get the groom here on time."

"Hey, Dezi. You're a sight for bloodshot eyes.

How's my favorite chef?" The sandy-blond-haired man swept the tray out of the woman's arms, leaned over and kissed her soundly on the lips.

"Oh, Grimm, be careful, or you'll dump the sliders." She braced her hands on her hips. "I've been up since before dawn, working hard to get this party started," she said. "And I'm relieved to see you all made it back from Bozeman with everyone."

Grimm laid the tray in the only empty spot on the conference table. "We had one job. And I'm happy to say we did it." He tipped his head toward the groom. "Murdock's here, a little worse for wear and maybe still a little drunk, but he's here."

Murdock pinched the bridge of his nose. "Not drunk. Hungover. They tried to kill me with shots last night." He dropped his hand and stared at the chef. "How's Gabbie?"

"Why?" the diminutive chef asked with a saucy tilt of her chin. "Are you worried she's gotten cold feet and changed her mind?"

Murdock's brows formed a V over his nose. "Did she?"

Dezi laughed. "Not a chance. She insisted on going to bed early so she wouldn't show up looking like death warmed over…like all of you." She leveled an accusing yet teasing stare at each man, stopping when she reached Liza and Tayla standing close to Utah. Her eyes widened. "And who do we have here?"

"That's right." The one called Grimm swung

toward Liza. "You were going to tell us your long story."

Everyone in the room turned toward Liza and Tayla.

An entire room full of people now knew she was there. Her pulse pumped hard through her veins as the urge to run nearly overwhelmed her. Liza inched toward Utah.

He leaned closer. "I trust every person in this room with my life," he said to Liza, his voice loud enough for the others to hear clearly. Then he turned to face them. "Guys, this is Liza." He nodded toward her. "And this old soul wrapped in a tiny package is Tayla." He plucked the beanie off Tayla's head. The messy bun slipped free of the elastic band Liza had used to hold it in place, and her long golden-blond, curls spilled down around her shoulders.

"Well, I'll be damn—" Grimm caught himself a little late and amended, "darned. I thought she was a *he*."

Liza pulled the baseball cap from her head and lifted her chin. "Look," she said. "We didn't come as wedding crashers. This is Murdock's big day. He and his bride should be the focus, not us. It's just that your guy, Utah, stopped to help us, and he hasn't been able to shake us since." She gave a crooked smile. "We'll just be going." Liza started for the door.

"Oh, no, no, no." Dezi, the chef, stepped in front of

Liza, her gaze on Utah. "Were these the guests you carried a tray to this morning?"

Utah nodded.

Liza forced a smile. "The breakfast was amazing. Thank you so much."

Dezi crossed her arms over her chest. "Spill it. We're not going anywhere until we know what's going on." She shot a glance toward Murdock. "If that's okay with our groom."

"That's right," Murdock said. "What did you do after you escorted us to our rooms last night?" He shook his head. "And I thought I'd had too much to drink. How did you end up with a woman and a child, and why did you just arrive in a helicopter?

Liza turned to Utah. "You might as well tell them," she said quietly.

Utah settled Tayla in a rolling chair, pushed it up to the table and filled a plate with a slider and some fruit before he straightened. "Here's what happened."

Ten minutes later, his teammates were all shaking their heads.

"Wow." Dezi approached Liza, tears in her eyes. To Liza's surprise, the chef reached out and hugged her hard. As she stepped back, she brushed a tear from her cheek. "I'm so sorry you went through all that. I'm going to make you both a special dessert."

"Do we need to postpone this wedding and go look for those people?" Murdock asked.

"No!" Everyone else in the room shouted.

Murdock wiped a hand across his forehead. "Good, because I really love Gabbie, and I want to spend the rest of my life with her. Starting today. Besides, we have a meeting with the social workers next week, and we need to be a married couple before they'll consider us fit to take in the two girls we rescued from the TCW."

"You rescued some girls from the TCW?" Liza looked up at Utah.

He nodded. "Another long story. I'll tell you about it after the wedding."

Liza's heart squeezed hard in her chest, realizing how much her presence was taking away from the groom's big day. She nodded to Murdock. "Tayla and I will get out of your way. This is your wedding day. I wish you and your bride all the love and happiness."

This time, when she started for the door, Dezi moved aside.

"Wait," Murdock called out. "Since you're here, you and Tayla should come to the wedding."

"That's right," Dezi said with a smile. "You should come to the wedding."

"I know Gabbie would want you to," Murdock said.

"That's very kind of you." Liza shook her head. "But you don't know me. This is a day for you and Gabbie. You should share it with your family and friends."

"We'd be honored if you'd join us. Besides, Utah

will be worried about you the whole time and ditch us the first chance he gets," Murdock said. "Come, if only so we can keep Utah longer than the ceremony."

Liza looked down at the clothes she wore. "We can't."

"Mommy, what is a wedding?" Tayla asked. "Can we go?"

Liza shook her head.

"If you're worried about what to wear," Molly said, "We'll find something for you." She tipped her head toward Tayla. "Hank and his wife are coming with their little ones. How old are you, Tayla?"

Tayla held up three fingers. "I'm three years old," she said.

Molly grinned. "Perfect. Hank's little girl is the same age. I'll call his wife Sadie and have her bring an extra dress and shoes."

"I really didn't want so many people to know where we are," Liza said. "Word will get out to the TCW. They're bound to be angry about my escape."

"And you're worried they'll come looking for you." Dezi nodded, then turned to the folks in the room. "Guys? Is anyone going to say anything to anyone outside our circle?" She shot a glance toward Liza. "Our circle includes Hank and his wife. Hank's safe. In fact, everyone coming to the wedding can be trusted." She touched Liza's arm. "You'll come?"

Tayla turned around and stood in her chair. "Please, Mommy?"

Liza knew it was a mistake, but then all these people already knew she was there. She looked up at Utah. "I'll need to leave afterward," she said.

Utah nodded. "I'll make sure you get somewhere safe."

Liza smiled at Tayla. "We're going to a wedding."

"Yay!" Tayla cried out and held out her arms to her mother.

Liza lifted her out of her chair and hugged her tightly. Tayla had never been to a wedding and really had no idea what one was. She'd be delighted with the dresses and music. Liza couldn't deny her daughter the experience.

"Now that we've got the scoop and it's settled that Liza and Tayla will join us, let's eat." Dezi glanced at her watch. "The photographer will be here in forty minutes, and the guys have to be in their tuxes by then." Dezi headed for the door. "Bon Appetit!"

"Wait," Grimm said. "Aren't you eating with us?"

Dezi shook her head with a grin. "I have a bridesmaid dress to get into. I'll see you when you walk me down the aisle." She winked. "It'll be good practice for our own wedding. Speaking of which, we need to set a date."

"You name it," Grimm said. "I'm ready."

"How's one month from today," Dezi shot back.

"Is that enough time for you to plan and get a dress?" Molly asked.

Dezi laughed. "Murdock and Gabbie pulled theirs

together in less than two weeks. I think we can do it in a month."

Molly chuckled and looked up at Parker. "Well?"

Parker held up his hands. "I was ready to say I do the day I asked you to marry me. Still am."

Molly's lips twisted. "And we got so busy renovating the lodge we haven't had time to plan our own wedding. I was using Murdock and Gabbie's nuptials as a dry-run for ours." She stepped into Parker's arms. "I want to have it as soon as we complete the remaining rooms. And I want it here at the Lucky Lady."

Parker kissed her. "Then let's get those rooms done. It's about time we got married and had those grandbabies your father's been after us to produce." He looked up. "If you'll excuse us, I have some kiss-the-bride practice to catch up on."

Molly giggled as Parker took her hand and led her out the door.

Liza ached to find the kind of love Molly and Parker and Dezi and Grimm clearly had for each other. Her chances of that happening were slim. Having escaped the TCW didn't mean the end of their hold on her and Tayla. They'd find her. Unless she kept moving. That kind of life left no room for love and weddings.

Utah handed her a plate. "Eat," he said. "You look like you could stand to put some meat on your bones." He winked. "Not that your bones aren't beautiful."

Liza might have to run again, but for one day, she could pretend she was a normal person, with nothing more to worry about than what dress to choose for a wedding. She loaded a plate full of the delicious food Dezi had prepared and found a seat close to Tayla and Utah.

For one day, she could pretend the three of them were a family.

She ate silently, watching Utah as he explained to Tayla what a wedding was.

He spoke to her as if she were an adult, never talking down to her or using baby talk. He smiled at her excitement when he told her they would dance after the wedding. He told her to save a dance for him.

Tayla nodded solemnly and promised she would.

Liza wondered if Utah would ask her to dance as well. The thought of him holding her close and swaying to music made her body tingle in anticipation.

Yes, she could pretend for one day that she was in love with this man who'd saved her life and treated her daughter with kindness and respect.

She pushed aside the danger this pretense brought with it.

The danger of actually falling in love with a man she would eventually have to leave behind.

CHAPTER 10

AFTER LUNCH, Utah walked Liza and Tayla back to his room, where he'd left his tuxedo hanging in the closet next to the shoes he'd wear with it.

"Are you going to join the guys in the conference room to get ready?" Liza asked.

Utah shook his head. "I'm not leaving you two alone."

"We'll be all right," Liza insisted. "You need to be with the groom. Besides, the photographer is coming to get snapshots of you getting him ready for the ceremony."

Utah shook his head. "They'll have to take photos without me. I'm getting ready here."

A knock sounded on the door.

Utah frowned. "I'll get it."

Liza swung her daughter up in her arms. "Come on, Tayla, let's wash your face and brush your teeth."

After she ducked into the bathroom, Utah looked through the peephole. Dezi stood on the other side.

Utah opened the door.

"I've come to get Liza and Tayla. The girls are all getting ready in the presidential suite. Gabbie brought a dress she thinks will fit Liza, and Molly sent her brother Bastian in with a stack of clothes for Tayla, including a dress for her to wear to the wedding. She said her daughter Emma is excited to meet Tayla." Dezi held up a hand. "And don't worry. They've all been sworn to secrecy." She looked past Utah. "Liza? Tayla?"

Liza emerged from the bathroom with Tayla in her arms.

"You're coming with me," Dezi said. "Us girls get to play fairy godmother." She held out her hand.

Liza looked to Utah.

"I'll walk with you to the suite. It's not far from the conference room."

Liza smiled. "Good. You can be with the groom."

Utah hadn't wanted to let Liza out of his sight, but she needed time to dress.

"I'll be surrounded by people," she insisted.

"We'll keep an eye on her," Dezi said. "Come on, ladies. We have to get beautiful."

Liza laid her hand in Dezi's and let her lead her into the hallway.

With his tux in one hand and his shoe box under

his arm, Utah followed behind the ladies to the beautifully remodeled presidential suite.

Dezi knocked on the door. "It's me, Dezi. I brought the others with me."

The door opened. Drake's fiancée, Cassie Douglas, stood there in her sheriff's deputy uniform.

Utah frowned. "Hey, Cassie, aren't you one of the bridesmaids?"

She nodded. "I am. I ended up having to pull a graveyard shift after the other girls went to bed. One of the guys had food poisoning and couldn't make it in." She smiled. "I can do without sleep. The girls assure me a little makeup will hide the dark shadows beneath my eyes. It's not every day a friend gets married."

She stepped aside. "Get in here, you guys. The others are armed to the teeth with makeup, curling irons and hairspray, ready to turn us all into princesses."

Tayla clapped her hands and waved at Utah as the women went inside.

Cassie met Utah's gaze. "I'll make sure they're safe," she assured him.

"Thank you," he said.

She closed the door, leaving Utah standing in the hallway.

For a moment, he considered staying there until the women emerged for the wedding. Then he shook his head. Cassie was a sheriff's deputy. Between her and Liza, who'd been trained as an assassin, they could hold their own. He doubted TCW people would make a play for Liza and Tayla while people surrounded them. As well, they weren't far from the conference room.

Utah joined the men down the hall and tried to act like his focus was on Murdock.

The photographer came into the room and took pictures of the groom with Drake, his best man, helping him adjust his bowtie.

They finished dressing, and the photographer had them move outside to take pictures in front of the lodge.

The entire time, Utah worried they were too far away from the women. He posed and forced a smile for the camera but kept his eye on the lodge throughout the ordeal.

The photographer finished with them and moved on to the presidential suite to take pictures of the women helping the bride get ready.

Utah returned to the conference room with the men and waited for the ceremony to begin.

Time might as well have stood still. The minutes crawled by.

Utah started for the door several times. Each time, Grimm stopped him, showing him the texts he was getting from Dezi.

The women had included Liza and Tayla in the

fun. They were getting their hair and makeup done, along with the bride and bridesmaids.

Only slightly relieved, Utah stayed put until Parker stepped into the room and announced, "It's time."

The men lined up in the hallway at the edge of the lobby.

The guests had been seated and waited for the ceremony to begin. One of Hank's Brotherhood Protectors had volunteered to man the music, claiming he'd earned spending money as a DJ in high school. He played muted music, waiting for the cue to start the song Gabbie had chosen for her walk down the aisle.

Utah scanned the faces of the men he'd met who worked for the Brotherhood Protectors. Most had brought along their wives or fiancées. Hank was seated close to the front with his wife, the megastar Sadie McClain. He held his baby boy in his lap with his little girl, Emma, seated between him and Sadie.

Utah searched for the blond heads of Liza and Tayla. When he didn't find them, his heart stilled and panic built.

Where were they?

Grimm tapped his arm. "You gotta see this." He tipped his head toward the hallway behind them.

Utah turned to find Liza and Tayla walking toward him, their blond hair curling softly around their shoulders.

Liza wore a pale blue dress that clung to her body, emphasizing the curves he'd known were hidden beneath the baggy clothes he'd found her in.

The dress flared out at the hips, swaying softly around her calves as she walked toward him in strappy silver sandals.

His breath caught and held in his throat.

Sweet Jesus, she was beautiful.

When she saw him, she smiled and pressed a hand to her chest. Her gaze swept his length, her eyes widening. Then she glanced down at Tayla.

The little girl's face was wreathed in a smile so bright it eclipsed the sun. She wore a soft pink dress made of material that floated around her like a cloud. It was accented with a matching wide satin sash tied around her middle.

When she saw Utah, she let go of her mother's hand and ran to him.

Utah swung her up in his arms and hugged her tightly. "You look like a fairy princess."

She hugged him around the neck, grinning. "I *am* a fairy princess. Miss Dezi said so." She twisted in his arms to look back. "And so is Mommy."

Utah held out a hand as Liza joined them and placed her palm in his. "Yes, Tayla, your mother is a fairy princess, too."

"You look amazing," Liza whispered.

"The boy cleans up well." Grimm grinned at Liza. "And so do you two. You're both beautiful."

Liza blushed. "Thank you."

To Utah, Grimm said, "You want to seat them before the procession starts?"

Tayla wiggled. "Put me down."

Utah lowered the child to the floor.

Liza smoothed Tayla's dress.

"Come with me to be seated for the ceremony." Utah caught Tayla's hand in his and held out his arm to her mother.

Liza slipped her hand into the crook of his elbow. As a unit, they moved down the aisle and found two empty seats behind Hank and Sadie.

Liza helped Tayla into her seat and sank into hers, leaning toward Sadie. "Thank you so much for the clothes for Tayla."

Sadie beamed at her. "It was my pleasure. The girls will have so much fun dancing tonight."

Happy to see Liza settled close to Hank, Utah excused himself and rejoined the groom.

Murdock squared his shoulders. "Ready?"

Utah laughed. "I should be asking *you* that."

"I've been ready," Murdock said. "Let's get this show on the road."

Drake straightened the groom's bowtie one more time.

"It's fine," Murdock said and stepped around him. He marched down the aisle to his position at the front of the rows of seats.

The groomsmen fell in step behind him, taking

their positions beside the groom.

Since Gabbie only had three bridesmaids, the fifth member of the team, Judge, had offered to conduct the ceremony, going so far as to apply online for a license to perform weddings. He took his position center stage.

The DJ switched to the song for the bridal procession.

One by one, the bridesmaids floated down the aisle and lined up across from the groomsmen.

Cassie stood across from Drake. Dezi was next, across from Grimm and Mollie McKinnon smiled at Utah.

The guests stood as Gabbie walked down the aisle, a vision in a white wedding dress that hugged her body down past her hips before flaring out like a mermaid's tail.

Murdock's eyes shone with moisture—his love for his bride there for all to witness.

Utah found himself envying the man's one hundred percent certainty of his commitment to Gabbie.

Utah's gaze sought Liza.

He'd never considered marriage, thinking he wasn't the kind of guy who would settle down with one woman for the rest of his life. Now, he stood as witness to his buddy's promise to love one woman until death and questioned his prior belief about himself. Could he be the kind of man who could fully commit to one woman for the duration of their lives?

His gaze on Liza, the idea didn't sound so farfetched as it had before he'd met the little assassin.

The ceremony was short. Judge did a good job leading them through their vows. They each had prepared additional declarations as well. After they'd made their promises and exchanged rings, Judge declared them husband and wife and gave them permission to kiss.

All that preparation, a brief promise and a kiss, was all there was to it. Murdock took his bride's hand and walked back down the aisle a married man, grinning like a fool.

Utah found himself wishing he could be that lucky. Was he truly done being a confirmed bachelor? Could he pledge himself to one woman for the rest of his life? Was he ready to have children?

If anyone had asked him those questions two days ago, he'd have laughed and told them absolutely not.

As he walked Molly back down the aisle, his gaze went to Liza and Tayla.

Could two strangers change him so completely and in such a short amount of time?

The answer was yes.

Though the ceremony was over, the photographer had another twenty minutes' worth of photos to take before the bridal party could join the others in the dining room where the reception dinner was served.

Hank and Sadie took Liza and Tayla under their

wing and ushered them into the dining room. The two little girls held hands all the way there.

Utah's heart warmed at how quickly Tayla had made a friend. She looked happy and carefree, like a three-year-old should be.

Once the photographer released them to move on to the dining room, Utah hurried ahead, anxious to get Liza and Tayla back in his sight.

He sat at a table with them and ate the meal Dezi had planned and prepared prior to her duties as a bridesmaid.

Drake gave his best man's toast, wishing Murdock and Gabbie a happy life together. Dezi toasted the union and wished their life together to be full of love and children.

They performed their dance together, and finally, the rest of the guests joined them on the floor.

Utah had been counting the minutes until he could dance with Liza. But first, he had promised a dance with Tayla.

He stood, bowed over her hand and asked, "Miss Tayla, would you do me the honor of dancing with me?"

Tayla giggled. "Yes, please."

He bowed again, then swept her up in his arms and waltzed her around the floor. She giggled and held on, pretending she was a princess and he was a handsome prince.

When little Emma wandered onto the dance floor, Tayla demanded that Utah set her on her feet. Emma took Tayla's hand, and the two little girls did their own version of a dance, smiling their happiness.

Utah returned to the table where Liza waited and held out his hand. "Ms. Liza, would you do me the honor of a dance?"

Her cheeks flushed a soft pink. "I would love to."

He swept her into his arms and whirled her around the floor, her skirt swirling around her legs. Finally, he slowed and held her close, resting his cheek against her soft hair. "You're beautiful."

She laughed. "So are you."

He smiled down at her. "Men aren't beautiful. They're handsome."

"No," she said. "I'm absolutely certain. You're beautiful."

His brow wrinkled. "I won't argue. Not when I'm holding the most stunning woman in the room." He went back to leaning his cheek against her hair.

"Tayla has a friend," Liza said with a sigh. "Oh, and Molly gave me the keys to the room beside yours. You can sleep in your own bed tonight."

He frowned. "I didn't mind sleeping outside your door. That way, I knew you weren't disturbed."

Liza grinned. "She mentioned a connecting door between your room and mine. It's behind the dresser."

His frown lifted. "Good. I can't protect you if I don't know what's happening."

She leaned up and pressed a kiss to his lips. "You don't have to protect us."

"Oh, yes, I do," he said.

At the end of the song, the bride had the single ladies line up for the bouquet toss.

Liza refused to get up in front of everyone to make a play for the bunch of flowers tied with ribbon.

Dezi caught the bouquet and held it up for Grimm to see. "One month."

He swung her around and dipped her low for a kiss. "We could fly to Vegas tomorrow."

She laughed, her cheeks flushed. "Tempting."

The groom seated his bride and slipped his hands beneath the hem of her dress to snag the garter from her leg. Drawing it down slowly, he slipped it off her ankle and held it up triumphantly.

The DJ called for the single men to line up to catch the garter.

"Go," Liza said.

Utah left her briefly, always keeping her and Tayla in sight.

So intently watching them, he didn't see when Murdock tossed the garter.

It landed on Utah's head, making everyone laugh. A smile tugged at his lips as he joined Liza, twirling the garter on a finger.

The bride and groom chose that moment to announce they were leaving, thanking the guests for coming and encouraging them to stay, dance and eat all the goodies Dezi had prepared.

As the bride and groom left the lobby, they were showered with birdseed. Then they climbed into a dark SUV and drove away to happy cheers.

"Mommy, I'm tired," Tayla raised her arms.

Utah lifted her in his arms. "Lay your head on my shoulder."

Tayla did. As they passed Hank and Sadie gathering their things, she looked up and waved at Emma.

Sadie smiled at Liza. "We need to set up a playdate for the girls."

Liza stiffened next to Utah. She answered. "That would be nice." Her voice was wooden and tight.

Utah wondered why she'd turned cold to Sadie, one of the nicest women he knew.

Utah carried Tayla with Liza at his side. When they were alone in the hallway, he asked. "Why did you stiffen when Sadie suggested you arrange a playdate?"

Liza sighed. "Tayla and I won't be around."

"If you weren't being threatened by the TCW, would you stay in Eagle Rock?"

Liza nodded. "I'd like that more than anything. These people have been so kind, including two strangers on their special day. You saw Tayla's face.

For the first time in her short life, she got to be a princess. I've never seen her so happy. I want her to have a lot more days like that. Full of joy and happiness."

They arrived in front of the door to Utah's room.

Liza pulled a key card from a hidden pocket in the frothy blue dress. "We should go to our room."

"Let me check both rooms before you go in." He handed Tayla to Liza and slid his key through the card reader. The green light blinked on, and he twisted the handle. He propped the door open to keep an eye on the two girls in the hall. After checking his room and the adjoining bathroom, he pushed the dresser away from the connecting door and unlocked his side.

"All good in there," he said.

Liza handed him her key card, and he entered her room, performing the same check and unlocking the connecting door from her side, pulling it open.

"Clear," he said. "You two can come in."

The room was much like his, with tasteful furnishings and a fluffy white comforter on the bed. Liza entered, closed and locked her door behind her. She carried Tayla to the bed and laid her on the comforter. The little girl was fast asleep, exhausted from a long day and more fun than she'd had in a long time.

Utah's heart squeezed hard in his chest.

If it were up to him, that little girl and her mother would have a lot more happy days ahead of them. He hurried into his room and closed and locked his door. He shrugged out of his tuxedo jacket, tossed it onto a chair and came back to stand in the connecting door.

"Did you see the stack of clothes Sadie McClain brought for Tayla?" Liza asked softly.

Utah entered the room to inspect the little outfits, amazed at the variety and bright colors. "Tayla will love wearing these," he said. The colors were as bright and cheerful as the child. How could one so young, who'd lived in such a harsh camp, be as happy and upbeat as Tayla?

"She's been a little trooper," Liza said. "I wanted so badly to get her out of there but was afraid they'd hurt her if I tried to escape. I could never have made it out without PJ's help."

"This PJ, is she one of the trainers or another one of the assassins?"

Liza hesitated while pulling a frilly sock off Tayla's foot. "She wasn't a trainer."

He nodded. PJ had been an assassin. "Had she been assigned a target yet?"

Liza frowned for a long moment and then nodded. "She said she didn't kill him, though. He died in a car accident before she got to him. They threatened to use Tayla to force me to make the kill. I wonder what or rather who they used to force PJ to go after her target." Liza looked down at her sleeping daughter. "I guess, once you've killed, you can't go back. You're a murderer. They know it and will use that against you as well." She looked up at Utah. "Did Hank get word to the congresswoman to be on the lookout for an attempt on her life?"

Utah nodded. "He had Swede pass on that information to their regional office in West Yellowstone."

She sighed. "They'll send someone else. They don't give up." Liza stared down at Tayla. "I'll do anything to keep my daughter safe. But killing someone?" She looked up, her gaze locking with Utah's.

He gripped her arms. "That's not who you are."

"No. It's not." She leaned her forehead against his white button-down shirt. "And it wasn't the example I wanted to set for my daughter. I'd never be able to look her in the eye. You know how she loves people. Even when we were imprisoned at The Camp, she saw the best in everyone around her. She would never forgive me."

Utah pulled her close. "You did the right thing by getting out."

Her fingers curled into the fabric of his shirt, her fingernails scraping his skin. The contact sent electric shocks skittering across his nerves.

"I couldn't have done it without PJ," she said. "Now, I can't even return the favor. I don't know where they've gone. I don't know if she's still alive..."

He stroked her back in long, even caresses, loving how soft yet muscular she was beneath the pale blue dress.

"How does an organization like the TCW persist?" she asked, looking up into his eyes.

He brushed his thumb across her cheek. "They're good at hiding. Montana isn't only known for its big sky. There are a lot of mountains, caves and hidden valleys where people can disappear indefinitely. Hank and his team are on it now. If anyone can find them, Hank's team can. Swede is a master at the computer. From what I've heard, he's good at hacking as well. There's not a database he can't tap into."

"They tend to live off the grid," she pointed out. "They ran the electricity off a generator."

"How did they give you your assignment? How did they tell you Congresswoman Lightfeather was your target?" He tipped her chin up and looked into her blue-eyed gaze.

"A computer tablet," she said.

"They had to have internet capability to show you Lightfeather's image on the tablet."

She nodded. "They had computers and monitors running off the generators and a portable satellite dish. You saw the camp. All that equipment, the stoves in the mess hall, beds from the bunk house, the generators, computers…everything. They were all gone when we got there today."

"Which means they took them to their next location. If they're on the internet, Swede will find them." Utah gave her a gentle smile. "And you need to sleep in case things go sideways anytime soon."

He bent and pressed a kiss to her forehead.

"Why did you do that?" she asked, her voice breathy, her eyes rounding.

"I don't know. It just felt…right."

She nodded, her eyes wide, her full lips slightly parted.

A strong urge to really kiss her washed over him, threatening to overwhelm him.

Liza was a beautiful woman. With her hair curling around her shoulders and the dress emphasizing the delicate curves of her body, she was irresistible.

Utah fought the desire building inside. He forced himself to remember where they were and who she was. This woman had been through so much at the hands of evil men. He didn't need to add to her trauma by making unwanted advances.

He stepped back, letting his arms fall to his sides. "Go to bed, Liza, before I do something we'll both regret."

He turned and walked away.

"Utah," she called out softly.

He stopped but didn't face her, afraid that if he did, he wouldn't be able to walk out of the room. "Yes?"

"Do what?" she whispered.

"Huh?" He faced her, a frown pulling his eyebrows downward. 'What do you mean by do what?"

She took a step toward him. "What would you do that we both might regret?"

CHAPTER 11

ANOTHER STEP BROUGHT Liza to stand in front of him. "I can't image regretting anything you might do." She laid a hand on his chest. "Were you going to do this?" Leaning up on her toes, she pressed her lips to his in a gentle kiss. She leaned back and stared up at him, an eyebrow cocked in challenge, her heart racing. Fear gripped her. Fear that she'd read him wrong. That he wasn't as attracted to her as she was to him.

He stood still, his hands at his sides.

Not ready to give up, she tried again. "Or something more like this?" she said, her voice husky. Her arms encircled his neck and brought him closer.

For a moment, she thought he would reject her advances. For a moment, her heart dropped to the pit of her belly.

Then Utah cupped the nape of her neck with one

hand and wrapped an arm around her back, drawing her as close as he could get her.

They'd have to be naked to stand any closer.

The thought of Utah naked made heat coil at Liza's center and spread throughout her body.

He deepened her kiss, pushed past her teeth and caressed her tongue. The sweetness of wedding cake and Utah made her want more.

Emboldened by his touch, Liza pressed her breasts against his chest and hooked one of her calves around the back of his thigh.

A soft sigh and the rustling of sheets pierced Liza's haze of desire, reminding her they weren't alone in the room. A small child slept nearby.

Utah lifted his head and stared down into Liza's eyes. "Maybe we should stop here. I don't want to start something that will make you uncomfortable after all you've been through."

She cupped his cheek and gave him a saucy smile. "You didn't start this."

He grinned. "True."

"And you have made me uncomfortable. A good kind of uncomfortable..." She frowned playfully, "if you leave me hanging."

His gaze went to the child sleeping with a hand tucked beneath her cheek.

"She sleeps hard for the first few hours." Liza looked up at him, her head tilted.

"Are you sure this is what you want and not just some way to thank me for saving your life?"

She reached for the bowtie around his neck and tugged it loose. "I've wanted this from the moment I saw you standing there in that tuxedo. I don't know why, but seeing you so formal after being confined in that dirty camp made my heart beat faster and my blood burn." She pulled the tie from around his neck and tossed it aside. "Now, if I'm making *you* uncomfortable, tell me." She paused with her hands on the top button of his shirt. "You might not feel the same way I do."

He grasped her face between his hands and stared into her eyes. "Sweetheart, do you feel like you'll explode if you don't kiss me, and you'll die if you don't strip every last item of clothing off your body and mine?"

Liza nodded, her tongue sweeping across her suddenly dry lips. "That's how I feel."

"Same," he said, his jaw tight. He lowered his head until their lips were a breath apart. "I want you so badly, I can barely breathe."

"Then what are we going to do about it?" She rose on her toes, closing the distance between their mouths.

He crushed her to him, claimed her lips and kissed her long and hard, diving deep to caress her tongue in long, sensuous strokes.

Kissing her was a start but not the end of what she wanted him to do.

The urgency of her need made her break the kiss. "I want you. Now. Inside me."

He bent and swept her into his arms, strode through the connecting door into his room and straight to the bed.

He set her on her feet and turned her slowly around, pressing his lips to the curve of her neck. His fingers found and pulled the zipper on the back of her dress, lowering it all the way down to the small of her back. He followed the zipper, brushing kisses against the exposed portion of her back.

Liza shivered, her need escalating with each touch of his lips and brush of his fingers against her skin.

Straightening, he pushed the straps over her shoulders.

Liza gave a little shimmy, and the dress slithered over her hips and pooled in a sea of light blue at her feet. She stepped out of the dress and turned to face him, wearing nothing but a pair of lacy white panties.

Utah moaned and reached for her.

She captured his hands in hers and shook her head. "Not yet." Liza reached up and flicked open the buttons on his shirt, working her way down his chest in swift, efficient movements until she reached the waistband of his trousers. She tugged the shirttail free and pushed it over his shoulders. It fell off his back but caught on his wrists. The look was sexy as hell, but he wasn't naked enough.

Liza made quick work of unbuttoning his cuffs, and the shirt joined her dress on the floor.

When she reached for the zipper on his trousers, Utah caught her hands. "Taking too long," he bit out. He toed off his shoes and shucked his trousers, boxers and socks.

When he finally stood naked before her, she smiled, took his hand and cupped her breast with his palm. Her eyelids closed, and she drew a deep breath, letting it out slowly.

He let her set the pace even though she wanted him to grab her up, toss her on the bed and make love, hard and fast. She respected him for that. But he'd nailed it.

Too slow.

Liza opened her eyes and stared up at him. "I wanted to take it slowly and commit everything to memory." She drew in another deep breath and let it out all at once. "But I can't. I want you so badly that slow is not an option."

"Thank God. Because I will explode if I don't have you. Now." He scooped her up, laid her across the bed and came down beside her. "But I want all of you and your release. I want to know that I make you as crazy as you make me." He kissed the side of her neck and flicked his tongue across the pulse beating wildly at the base of her throat.

"You already make me crazy with wanting you," she said.

"Then let me make you crazier." Utah leaned up on his hands and bent over her, trailing kisses across her shoulders, her collarbone and lower. He swept a tongue across one of her nipples, setting fire to her nerve endings. The tip tightened into a hard little nubbin.

Liza sucked in a breath, her chest rising.

He sucked the breast into his mouth and pulled gently, alternating between flicking the tip with his tongue and rolling it across his teeth.

Her breathing grew ragged, and her core heated as he moved from one breast to the other and treated it to the same sensuous teasing.

When he moved lower, Liza's breaths came in short gasps, anticipation building, muscles tensing.

His hand slid between her legs and cupped her sex, his finger dipping into her slick channel.

Liza writhed beneath him, the crazy he'd promised in full force, making her hips buck.

Utah parted her folds and swept his tongue over her clit.

Liza moaned and tensed as sparks ripped through her senses, setting her body on fire. She reached for his head, her fingers sliding into his hair, pulling him closer, urging him to do more, take more, make her burn.

He flicked her again and again.

The pressure inside intensified, growing until it exploded in a kaleidoscope of sensations, blasting through every inch of her body.

Her hips rocked, milking the feeling, riding it all the way to the end.

When she fell back to the mattress, she still ached for more. Liza gripped his arms and pulled. "Inside. Now."

He chuckled and climbed up her body, pausing to kiss her. Then he leaned over the side of the bed, opened the drawer on the nightstand and rummaged inside. When he found what he was looking for, he rose on his knees and tore open a packet.

Liza took the condom from him and rolled it down over his cock. Holy hell, he was big and hard.

For her.

Cloaked, he dropped down and kissed her again, his cock nudging her damp entrance.

He deepened the kiss and pressed into her slowly, allowing her channel time to adjust to his size.

Once he was all the way in, he held steady, breathing in and out.

Liza could tell he was holding tightly to his control. She wanted him to lose that control.

Grabbing his hips, she pushed him out and pulled him back in, setting the pace, increasing the speed and intensity with each pass.

He took over, pumping hard and fast.

Liza raised her knees, dug her heels into the

mattress and raised her hips to meet each thrust, sending him deeper.

When his body tensed, hers tensed. She twisted her hands in the comforter, rocked up and shot over the edge, her orgasm rippling through her in waves.

Utah thrust one last time, going deep. He threw back his head as he came, his cock pulsing in her channel.

They rode their releases together, coming back to earth in a tangle of blankets and sweat.

Utah kissed Liza, stealing her breath away with his tenderness. Then he rolled to his side, taking her with him.

For a long moment, they lay in each other's arms.

Liza loved the feeling of him still inside her and lying skin to skin. She embraced the joy of the moment, trying not to think beyond it.

As their passion cooled, so did her skin, bringing her back to reality. She stole a glance toward the open connecting door.

"We should dress," Utah said.

Liza pressed closér to him. "I know. I'm not sure how Tayla would react to finding us this way."

Utah chuckled. "I'd rather not put her to the test."

They rose from the bed, ducked into the bathroom and quickly rinsed in the shower. Utah wrapped her in a towel and sent her to her room with one of his T-shirts.

Liza dried her body and pulled the T-shirt over

her head. The soft cotton felt delicious against her sensitized skin. Knowing it was a shirt Utah had worn made it even better. She climbed into the bed with Tayla and pulled the comforter over her daughter and herself.

A shadow in the connecting door made her heart flutter.

Utah entered, wearing shorts and nothing else. He crossed to the bed and bent to brush a kiss across her lips. "Just so you know. I don't consider what happened to be a one-night-stand."

She looped her hand behind his head and brought him down for another kiss wanting to believe him, knowing it couldn't be so.

She was fooling herself if she thought she could stay there with Utah. The people who'd held her captive for ten months wouldn't let her go that easily.

"What happened was beautiful," she whispered.

His eyes narrowed briefly, but he didn't push. "Sleep. We'll figure things out in the morning."

Her gaze followed him until he disappeared into the other room. He was so close, but so far out of Liza's reach, it hurt her heart.

She lay next to Tayla, knowing her time with Utah was nearing an end. She'd have to move on soon or risk her own life and, more importantly, the life of her daughter.

CHAPTER 12

Utah lay for a long time, staring at the ceiling in the dark, listening for any little sound coming from the other room.

He wanted to go to Liza and hold her in his arms all night long. When he'd told her their lovemaking wasn't a one-night-stand, he'd meant that he didn't want it to end there. In the short time they'd been together, he'd fallen under her spell.

She was a beautiful woman, a dedicated, loving mother and a survivor.

And their passion had been off the charts.

He knew she was planning on running. The only way to stop her from doing that would be to bring down the entire TCW organization. If the network was as widespread as Liza believed, bringing them down would be nearly impossible. But, if they could capture the people in charge, the rest of the organization might collapse.

Cut off the head of the snake.

Bringing TCW down was the only way he'd keep Liza from leaving. Until that happened, she wouldn't feel safe unless she got herself and Tayla far away from Montana. Even then, they might not be safe.

He couldn't do much until morning, but then, he planned to go to Hank and come up with a plan. And if Utah couldn't convince Liza to stay, he'd damn well go with her.

He'd never believed in love at first sight. Hell, he hadn't believed much in love.

Something about Liza and Tayla made him reevaluate his previous views on love. Not that he could possibly be in love with Liza so soon. If he was capable of falling in love, she was the woman with whom he could see it happening.

He'd never much cared for children, not having been much of a child himself. Since meeting the intrepid Tayla with her bright and cheerful personality, he could grow to love that kid, if he didn't already. The thought of anyone hurting her, or threatening to hurt her to coerce her mother into doing something horrific, made him so angry he wanted to find those bastards and pound them into the ground.

Utah dozed off and woke to the sound of his phone ringing.

He fumbled for the device, read the caller ID and answered. "What's up, Hank?"

"Someone tried to kill Congresswoman Lightfeather early this morning."

Utah sat up. "Were you able to warn her?"

"Yes, we got word to our guys in the Yellowstone office, and they let her know. Fortunately, she's engaged to one of the Protectors. He was able to successfully defend her."

Movement caught Utah's attention.

Liza stood in the connecting door, wearing the T-shirt he'd given her, her blond hair tangled and so adorable, he wanted to kiss her.

Utah put his cell phone on speaker.

"Hank, I have Liza with me."

"Good morning, Liza."

"Hank," she acknowledged.

"What about the congresswoman?" Utah met Liza's gaze and held it. "Did she sustain any injuries in the attack?"

Liza crossed the room to stand beside Utah's bed.

"Lightfeather is fine," Hank said. "Shaken, not injured."

Utah held out his hand.

Liza put hers in his and sat on the side of the bed next to Utah.

"Did they catch the attacker?" Liza asked.

"No, ma'am," Hank said. "Our man, Dax, shot the guy, injuring him, but he got away. A sheriff's deputy found the attacker a couple of hours later, lying on the side of the highway with several more wounds than what Dax inflicted."

"Dead, I take it," Utah surmised.

"Very much so," Hank reported.

Liza squeezed Utah's hand. "They'll be back."

"Dax will be ready," Hank assured her. "I called to catch you up on the congresswoman and to run something by you both."

Utah exchanged glances with Liza. "Shoot."

"Sadie is worried about you, Liza and Tayla. Frankly, so am I. I know Utah can protect you, but we haven't been able to locate them, and we're worried they'll make a play for you and your daughter."

"I'm worried as well," Liza said softly. "Though it was fun to go to the wedding yesterday, and the accommodations at the lodge are great, I think it might be time for us to disappear."

Utah's gut knotted, and his hand tightened around Liza's. He didn't want to let them go.

"I thought you might be thinking along those lines. I want to give you another option." Hank paused. "Sadie and I would like you to come to stay at the White Oak Ranch with us. The security is a lot tighter here. We'd want Utah to come with you to provide one more layer of protection. You'd be safe, Tayla and Emma could play, and I'd have a chance to talk Utah into joining my team of Brotherhood Protectors."

Liza frowned. "I'd be afraid the people after me might hurt you and your family."

"They won't get past my security system," Hank said. "My family will be safe. Sadie and I would feel better knowing you and Tayla weren't on the run with nowhere to go and no protection."

Liza's eyes filled with tears. "I don't know what to say…"

Utah's heart filled with joy at the thought of spending more time with Liza and Tayla. More time for Liza to learn to trust him and for him to explore his growing feelings for Liza and Tayla. "Say yes," he whispered and held his breath, praying she would.

Liza stared at Utah's cell phone for several long heartbeats.

Just when Utah's hope waned, Liza met his gaze. "Okay. I'll come as long as Utah comes with us."

"Absolutely," Hank said. "You heard that, Utah. I'll make a Brotherhood Protector out of you yet."

"When do you want us out there?" Utah asked.

Hank chuckled. "The sooner, the better."

"We'll head that way after breakfast," Utah said.

"I'll let Sadie know the good news. Emma will be beside herself. And we can put our heads together to find and put a stop to these domestic terrorists."

"I'll help any way I can." Anything to stop them from targeting Liza and Tayla.

"All right, then. I'll see the three of you in an hour or two." Hank ended the call.

Utah brought Liza's hand to his lips and kissed the backs of her knuckles. "Are you okay with the arrangement?"

"As long as Hank's security is as robust as he says it is." She smiled. "Tayla will be thrilled. She enjoyed playing with someone her own age last night."

"Then let's get dressed, have some of Dezi's gourmet breakfast and get on the road to Hank's."

"I'll feel better once we get there." She grinned. "I can't wait to see Tayla's reaction when we tell her she gets to stay at Emma's house."

"Mommy?" Tayla appeared in the connecting doorway, barefoot, wearing a pretty blue nightgown dotted with fluffy white lambs in the shapes of clouds. She yawned big enough to split her face and then frowned. "You left me."

Liza opened her arms. "No, baby. I was right here."

Tayla ran into her mother's arms.

Liza hugged her close and then rolled over onto the bed next to Utah, with Tayla landing between them.

Utah tickled her sides and kissed her cheek. "Did you have fun at the wedding yesterday, little lamb?"

Tayla giggled and squirmed. "Yes. Me and Emma danced to music."

Utah laid back against the pillows, crossing his

arms behind his head. "Did you like playing with Emma?"

"Yes, yes, yes." Tayla laid back against the pillow and crossed her arms behind her head.

Utah chuckled, understanding the old saying that imitation was the best kind of compliment. His heart warmed lying beside Tayla with Liza on the other side, grinning at the two of them.

"How would you like to see Emma again?" Liza asked.

Tayla popped up to a sitting position. "Can we?"

Liza nodded. "We're going to stay at Emma's house for a while."

Tayla's eyes widened. "You, me and Utah?"

Again, Liza nodded.

"Yay!" Tayla clapped her hands and bounced up and down. Then she fell back against the pillow, staring up at the ceiling, smiling. A moment passed, and her smile turned to a frown. "Will the bad men from The Camp be able to find us there?"

Utah's heart squeezed hard in his chest at the fear in the little girl's eyes. He leaned on an elbow and smoothed a strand of the child's hair back from her forehead. "It's safe there. And you'll have me and your mama looking out for you."

Tayla's gaze shifted from Utah to her mother and back to Utah. "Can I take my new clothes?"

Liza laughed. "Of course, you can. And you can thank Emma and Ms. Sadie for giving them to you."

Tayla took one of Utah's hands and one of her mother's and pressed them to her cheeks. "This is the best day ever."

"Let's make it even better by having breakfast, and then we can go to Emma's." Liza leaped out of bed, grabbed Tayla and swung her up in her arms. "Come on, girlfriend. We have things to pack."

Utah smiled as Liza and Tayla crossed into the adjoining room. The warmth in his chest was the best feeling he'd had...ever. For a moment, he'd felt a part of Liza and Tayla's family. And he'd loved it. How would it feel to make that permanent? For Liza to be his wife and Tayla to call him Daddy?

His heart swelled in his chest.

For a guy who hadn't really liked the idea of marriage and children, he'd done a complete about-face.

Then again, who wouldn't with a kid like Tayla and a woman as strong, loving and beautiful inside and out as Liza?

He swung his legs over the side of the bed and got busy dressing quickly and packing his stuff. He found an empty gym bag and carried it into the other room. "You might want this."

Liza smiled, leaned up on her toes and brushed his lips with a kiss. "Thank you."

He caught her around her middle and crushed her to him, kissing her good and proper.

When he set her back on her feet, she laughed, her cheeks pink.

A little arm wrapped around one of Utah's legs. He glanced down at Tayla.

She'd wrapped an arm around her mother's leg as well and grinned up at them. "I like when we're a family."

Liza shot a wide-eyed glance at Utah.

He winked and ruffled Tayla's hair. "Me, too, baby." He left them to pack their meager belongings and finished jamming everything he owned into his duffel bag.

Liza entered the room wearing the jeans she'd escaped in and his T-shirt knotted at her hip. Tayla had on a pair of colorful leggings and a matching T-shirt. Her hair was pulled up on top of her head in a ponytail.

"Do you want to eat in the dining room or here in this room?"

Liza sighed. "After the wedding yesterday, I don't think it's a secret that we're here. Let's eat in the dining room. Then we can get to Hank's place, where we'll be safer."

Dezi was talking to one of the guests in the dining room when Utah, Liza and Tayla entered.

She grinned, excused herself and met them halfway across the room. "You're just in time. I was just about to put on a fresh batch of Belgian waffles. You can have whatever toppings your hearts desire. My personal favorite is strawberries and freshly whipped cream. We have chocolate, blueberries and maple syrup."

"Can we help?" Liza asked.

Dezi grinned. "Of course. I can always use another assistant in the kitchen."

They spent the next thirty minutes making waffles and smothering them in the toppings of their choice. Dezi made Tayla's day by outfitting her with her own chef's apron and hat. The fun continued into the dining room when Dezi joined them for breakfast, entertaining them with stories about growing up on the Double Diamond Ranch, where her father had been the foreman. She went on to regale them with some of the mischief she and her friends, Cassie, Gabbie and Penny, got into as teens.

At the mention of Penny, Dezi frowned and looked across the table at Liza. "You were in one of those camps run by The Chosen Way, weren't you?"

Utah could feel Liza stiffen beside him. Some of the sunshine faded from her face as she nodded.

Dezi leaned forward. "We recently learned that my friend Penny was one of the people held hostage. You see, she disappeared almost five months ago, and we haven't seen or heard from her since. I don't suppose you ran into her?" She pinned Liza with her hopeful gaze.

Liza shook her head. "In the camp where we were held, we weren't allowed to say our true names.

Instead, we were given names, and that's what we called each other." She gave Dezi a crooked smile. "They called me Fly."

Dezi's brow puckered. "Fly?"

Liza shrugged. "I was Fly for the past ten months. Even the trainers and the man in charge went by call signs or nicknames. Spike was my trainer. The guy in charge was Commander. The recruit who helped me escape was PJ. So, you see, if she was there, I wouldn't have known her by the name Penny."

Dezi sighed. "She was blond, like you, but her hair was more sandy than golden. She was shorter than you, an inch taller than me."

"There were a couple of women who could fit that description. PJ was one of them."

Dezi's eyes narrowed. "P for Penny?"

Liza touched Dezi's hand. "Even if PJ is your Penny, they've moved everyone who was there."

The chef's hopeful look fell. "Yeah, but it would be nice to know she's still alive. Hank and his team have been trying to find them since they busted up the other location. I just know it's only a matter of time before they find them and bring Penny back home to us."

"I'll help in any way I can," Liza said. "I want PJ out of there as well. She got us out when I didn't think it was possible. Do you have a picture of Penny?"

Dezi smiled. "I do." She pulled out her cell phone

and scrolled through, stopping at a photograph of four young women.

Liza recognized Dezi's brown hair, brown eyes and perky smile. She studied each face stopping at the two women of the same height. One had auburn hair and green eyes, the other had sandy blond hair and brown eyes. Both were smiling and happy.

She pointed at the blonde. "Is this your Penny?"

Dezi nodded. "Penny was the kind of person who made the impossible happen."

PJ had done the same. Still, she'd never seen PJ smile. Penny and PJ could be the same person, but she just didn't know for certain. "It's hard to say."

Dezi sighed. "I like to think your PJ is our Penny, and she's out there, not too far away."

The chef pushed back from the table. "And now, I have work to do. You'll love being out at Hank and Sadie's. The ranch is gorgeous, and the house is perfect." She gathered dishes and headed for the kitchen.

Utah, Liza and Tayla helped by carrying their empty plates and cups to the big sink.

"I'll take it from here," Dezi said. "You three need to get moving."

Utah thanked Dezi and ushered Liza and Tayla back to their rooms. Utah gathered their bags. Liza carried the gun Utah had given her the night he'd saved her life, and they left through the side door.

While Utah loaded their bags into the back seat,

Liza slid the gun into the glove box and closed it. She had just turned to help Tayla into the truck when an older woman rushed up to them, wild-eyed and frantic. "Help me. Oh, please help me!"

Liza gripped the woman's arm. "What's wrong?"

The woman turned toward a car in the far corner of the parking lot. Dark smoke rose from the rear of the vehicle.

"My husband came out earlier. I was still packing. He's in that car. There's smoke, and the doors are locked. He has the key inside. I pounded on the window, but he didn't respond. Help him! Please!"

Utah glanced around. No other people were standing in the parking lot. A blue repair van stood near the entrance to the lodge with Town & Country Heat and Air written in bold red letters across the side.

A couple of workers in blue coveralls were entering the lodge. The doors closed behind them before Utah could yell for their attention.

He turned to Liza. "You and Tayla get in the truck and lock the doors." He reached behind the back seat and grabbed the tire iron. "I'll be right back."

Liza nodded and helped Tayla up into the truck.

Once Liza was inside and the doors locked, Utah ran toward the smoking vehicle.

The man inside lay slumped against the steering wheel. Like the woman had said, the doors were locked from the inside.

Smoke poured from the back of the vehicle. With the possibility of whatever was causing the smoke igniting the fuel in the gas tank, Utah didn't have time to spare. He slammed the tire iron against the back window, shattering the glass. He reached inside toward the driver's door, fumbling for the door lock button.

The wind shifted, blowing the smoke toward Utah. He coughed and hit every button his fingers touched. After he thought he'd hit everything, he landed on a button, heard a loud click and the door unlocked.

Utah yanked open the door and reached inside. The old man lay with his cheek against the steering wheel, unresponsive.

Utah tried to drag him out and was stopped by a buckled seatbelt holding the man in. Not breathing, Utah leaned in, jabbed the release and leaned the man back to remove the shoulder strap.

With the smoke getting worse, Utah hooked the man beneath his shoulders and dragged him out of the vehicle and across the ground.

As he laid the man on the pavement, the car behind him exploded.

The blast threw Utah several feet in the air. He landed hard, hit his head on the asphalt and blacked out.

CHAPTER 13

Liza watched in horror as Utah struggled to reach the man in the vehicle. He raised the tire iron and slammed it against the back window.

At the same time as he hit that window, a loud crash sounded behind Liza, and splinters of glass flew across the cab.

She spun toward the sound.

A man in blue coveralls with a tire iron in one hand reached through the driver's window and unlocked the truck.

"What the hell!" Liza yelled and reached for the gun she'd tucked into the glove box. Before she could get her hand around the grip, her door flew open, and a big meaty hand grabbed her arm and dragged her out of the cab.

Liza opened her mouth to scream, but a hand clamped over her mouth.

The blue van that had been near the entrance a moment before rolled to a stop, blocking her view of the smoking vehicle and Utah.

Liza twisted and fought with every ounce of her strength and cunning. The arm around her was like an iron band. Like the nightmare of her first abduction, she was carried into the waiting van. The man holding her climbed in with her.

The other man who'd busted the window was right behind them, carrying Liza's squirming daughter, who was fighting as fiercely as Liza.

As the man carrying Tayla stepped up into the van, Tayla wiggled free and dropped to the ground. Instead of running away, she launched herself at the man holding onto Liza. "Leave my Mommy alone!"

At that moment, a loud explosion rocked the van.

The man behind Tayla scooped her up, dove into the van and slid the side door shut. As the van spun around, Liza could see flames shooting up from what was left of the vehicle Utah had been working beside moments before.

Her heart stopped beating for a full five seconds and then slammed hard against her ribs. No. Utah was okay. He had to be. He'd promised her that last night wasn't a one-night stand. That meant he'd be around for a while, didn't it?

She twisted as best she could, searching for Tayla.

Her daughter was held tightly against the man wearing blue coveralls. The cap he'd worn had been knocked from his slick, bald head. He looked across the van at her, his lips pulling back in a sneer. "Hey, Fly. You didn't think I'd forget about my favorite recruit and her brat, did you?"

Her heart sank into the pit of her belly, where it roiled and pitched.

The hand over her mouth moved, but the arm around her remained firm, pinning her arms to her sides.

"Spike."

"Did you miss me?" he leered. "I missed you. We all missed you. Especially Skeeter. He got tagged with your assignment when you decided to take one of our trucks for a joy ride."

Liza's chest tightened. Skeeter had been one of the young men who'd trained alongside her and PJ. He'd been young and impressionable enough that they'd managed to brainwash him into believing he was one of them in the fight to save the country from rotting from the inside. He couldn't have been more than eighteen or nineteen years old. A kid.

His was the body the sheriff had found on the side of the road with more bullets in him than the one Dax had hit him with.

"You killed him," she said.

"He failed his first assignment, and his face was seen by too many people." Spike shrugged. "He was of no further use to us and a liability if he was caught.

We can't leave loose threads lying around, now, can we?"

"Is that what we are?" Liza shook her head. "Do what you want with me, but let my daughter go. She's only three years old."

"A perfect age to begin training. They're like clay that can be shaped and formed any way we need."

"I'm not clay," Tayla said. "Let my Mommy go."

Liza hoped they wouldn't kill them quickly and dump them on the side of the road like Skeeter. She needed time to come up with an escape plan. She'd be on her own this time, without PJ's help. But, damn it, she had to do it. Tayla deserved a life longer than three short years, and Liza wanted to be with Utah again. She prayed he hadn't been injured when the car had exploded. "What are you going to do with us?"

"Well, now, that's totally up to you." Spike's eyes narrowed. "Your target is still alive and well and poisoning this country with her lies."

"And you expect me to eliminate the target," she said, her tone as dead as her heart.

"It's simple. You take out the target, and you get your daughter back." Holding Tayla clamped under one arm, Spike dug into a pocket of his overalls and pulled out a burner cell phone. "This is your lifeline to your daughter. You have twenty-four hours to get it done. At that time, you'll receive a call letting you know where you can find your brat. You show up with proof that you did it, and you'll get your daughter."

"How do I know you won't do to me what you did to Skeeter?"

"Easy," Spike said. "Don't be seen, and don't get shot." With his free hand, he smacked the back of the driver's seat.

The van skidded to a stop on the side of the road.

The man holding Liza yanked open the sliding door and shoved her out.

As she scrambled to her feet, Spike shouted, "Twenty-four hours begins now."

"Mommy!" Tayla cried.

The door slid shut, and the van sped off, kicking up gravel in its wake.

"Tayla!" Liza ran after the van, tears streaming from her eyes. The van disappeared around a curve in the road.

Liza staggered to a stop and bent double, sobs wracking her body. "My baby."

The echo of Spike's voice cut through her grief.

Twenty-four hours.

Liza straightened and scrubbed the tears from her eyes. Twenty-four hours was barely enough time to get to wherever Congresswoman Lightfeather might be.

Liza's breath lodged in her lungs. What if congress was in session, and Liliana Lightfeather had flown to Washington, D.C.? Could Liza get there and do the job in the time allotted?

Not that she considered killing the woman. But she had to do something. She needed a plan. She needed help, and she wouldn't find it running after the van carrying her daughter farther away with each passing second.

An image of Tayla's stricken face and the sound of her voice crying out made Liza's heart ache so badly that she pressed a hand to her chest. The only thing that would ease the pain was to get her daughter back.

She turned around and headed back the way they'd come. How far was it back to the lodge? The van had been moving fast. They could have gone a couple of miles before they dumped her on the side of the road. A couple of miles on foot took time to cover. She didn't have much time.

Liza walked faster and faster until she was running. Time was the enemy. She didn't have nearly enough to do whatever had to be done.

And if she didn't do what they wanted, she'd never see her daughter again.

She stared at the burner phone in her hand. Her only link to her daughter. "Oh, Tayla," she whispered. "Hang on, baby. I'm coming for you."

She'd been running for a couple of minutes when she came to a curve in the road. Halfway around that curve, a vehicle appeared, coming from the opposite direction. It was a truck, and it was moving so fast it skidded sideways before it straightened. The driver must have spotted her because its brakes squealed, and the vehicle slid to a stop.

The door swung open, and the driver leaped out.

"Utah!" Liza ran into his arms.

He held her close. "Tayla?"

"They took her," Liza said. "They took my baby. I have twenty-four hours." She looked up into his eyes, her tears drying. "I have twenty-four hours to kill the congresswoman, or I'll never see Tayla again. I need to move." She stepped out of his embrace and raced toward his truck.

She dove into the passenger seat.

Utah leaped into the driver's seat and slammed the door with the busted window. "We need to get to Hank's. He'll know what to do."

"I need to get to Wyoming or wherever Liliana Lightfeather is."

"Hank can get you there faster. With his help, we'll come up with a plan and the means to execute it."

She sat in her seat, trying not to think of how scared Tayla was or what they might do to her if Liza failed to give them what they wanted.

She glanced at Utah and noted blood on his forehead. "You're hurt."

He shook his head. "Just a scratch."

"The explosion?" she asked.

He nodded. "Luckily, I got the man out of the car before it went off."

"Good." She reached across the console and touched his arm. "I'm glad you're okay."

His gaze met hers. "I'm sorry."

"For what?"

"That I didn't see it coming." He stared straight ahead, his jaw hard, his hands gripping the steering wheel so tightly his knuckles turned white. "I wasn't there for you and Tayla."

She shook her head. "You had to get that man out of the car. If you hadn't gotten him out when you did, he would've died in that explosion. Hell, I thought we were safe inside the truck."

"And you weren't." He glanced her way. "I died a thousand deaths when I looked up and the truck was empty."

"I didn't know if you were dead or alive. You were still working on getting into that man's car the last time I saw you. Then I saw the car on fire after the explosion as we left the parking lot." She shook her head. "I didn't know."

He reached for her hand. "We'll get her back."

She nodded, praying he was right.

As they passed through Eagle Rock, Utah called Hank, giving him a heads-up about what had happened and what they needed to make happen within Liza's timeframe. He broke every speed limit getting to the White Oak Ranch.

Ten precious minutes later, they pulled up to Hank's ranch house.

Hank was waiting on the porch. He held the door for Utah and Liza and directed them to the Brotherhood Protectors war room in the basement.

Swede was there, hands on his keyboard.

"Do you have them on the comm?" Hank asked.

Swede nodded. "Got 'em." He touched the keys, and an image materialized on the big screen at the end of a long conference table.

Two faces appeared. A man with brown hair, blue eyes and a neatly trimmed beard. Beside him was Congresswoman Liliana Lightfeather.

Liza pressed a hand to her chest. This was the woman she'd been ordered to kill. Seeing her alive and in real-time made it even more impossible to follow through with the order to assassinate the woman.

Hank waved a hand toward the screen. "Dax Young and Congresswoman Lightfeather, this is Pierce Turner and Liza Gray."

"Please, call me Liliana," the woman with coal-black hair and brown-black eyes met Liza's gaze. "I hear you've been tasked with the dubious job of killing me."

Liza looked straight into the woman's eyes. "I have twenty-three hours and forty-two minutes until they contact me. I need to have proof that I've completed the job, or I'll never see my daughter again."

Liliana drew in a breath and let it out slowly. "I can tell you now that I don't want to die any more than you want to kill me. Dax, Hank, Swede and I discussed the options and think we've come up with an alternative plan." She shifted her gaze to Hank. "You want to lay it out?"

Hank nodded. "My Yellowstone team is in place, providing twenty-four-seven surveillance and protection since the first attempt on Ms. Lightfeather's life. They know of four men currently watching the safe house she's been taken to. They won't get within fifty yards of the building. Our team won't let them. But, they're watching. And they'll bear witness to anyone who manages to get past our team."

Liza's brow furrowed. "The proof I need?"

Hank grimaced. "Not completely. But witnesses that will let the people holding Tayla know you made it in.

Liza nodded. "And how am I supposed to kill Ms. Lightfeather?"

"Liliana," the congresswoman insisted with a crooked smile. "I'm hoping you won't kill me."

Liza made no promises, waiting for Hank to continue as the clock ticked away the minutes.

"You'll make your way to the safe house near West Yellowstone. We'll make it look like you got there on your own, hitching a ride in the back of a tractor-trailer rig. We'll arrange a car for you to steal at a truck stop in West Yellowstone and leave an AR-15 semi-automatic rifle in the trunk. You'll drive to the safe house, stop half a mile from the location and wait."

"I'm supposed to attend a dedication ceremony tomorrow for the new Wind River Reservation community center," Liliana said. "We'll let it slip that I'll be moving under the cover of night from the safe house to my home on the rez."

"A vehicle will leave the safe house at two o'clock in the morning. You'll be in position on the side of the road. When the car approaches, you'll fire on it, aiming high to give the driver time to dive out the side into the ditch."

Dax held up a hand. "That would be me. I'd appreciate it if you didn't shoot me."

Liza's brow twisted. "You trust me?"

"I'm not your target," Dax said. "And Liliana won't be in the vehicle. You have no reason to kill me."

"Why should the watchers believe Liliana is in that vehicle?"

"We'll have my team converge on the site and call for an ambulance," Hank said.

"They'll pull two dummies out of the vehicle and load them into the back of the ambulance. The bodies will arrive at the coroners' office where their information will be logged into the system, care of our computer magician." Hank waved toward Swede.

"They'll come complete with photographs of the deceased and a death certificate."

Liza shook her head. "It's too complicated."

"It's what we have short of actually pulling the trigger on Ms. Lightfeather," Hank said.

"She can't stay dead forever," Liza pointed out.

"No, but I can stay dead long enough for you to make them think I am," Liliana said.

Dax leaned forward. "We want you to get your daughter back. If it takes being declared dead for a few days, it's better than actually being dead."

"What if they renege on their promise and don't show up with my daughter?"

Hank turned to Swede. "Tell them."

The big blond guy faced Liza. "You have less than twenty-four hours to do what they've asked. We need that time to get into place."

"Into what place?" Liza demanded.

Swede met and held her gaze. "We think we've found where they've moved."

Liza's heart stilled, and then anger burned to the surface. "If you've found them, why go to the trouble of staging Liliana's death? Why not mobilize the National Guard and go straight to that location? You could rescue my daughter and capture the bastards, putting an end to their brand of terrorism."

"It's complicated," Swede said. "We don't know that they have your daughter there. Until they arrange for you to meet them and provide proof, we don't know where they're keeping her."

"We will have our people in place to raid the camp," Hank said.

"And I'll be tapped into your phone," Swede continued, "ready to trace the incoming call's location. You'll demand proof of life before you agree to meet them. Keep them on the line as long as you can so that I can triangulate the signal and get their exact location. That'll get us to your daughter."

Hank touched Liza's arm. "We won't move on the compound until your daughter is safe."

"You're assuming they'll actually let me near her. What if they ghost me?"

"When you prove to them you did what they demanded, they'll want you to do it again," Hank said. "They'll lure you back into the fold, using your daughter as collateral."

"And if I don't prove that I killed Liliana," Liza's shoulders sagged. "They'll eliminate me like they did Skeeter. He was of no more use to them."

Hank and Swede nodded.

Utah slipped an arm around Liza's waist. "You have to prove the kill."

Liza looked up into his eyes. "Where will you be?"

"If not with you," Utah said, "I'll be pretty damned close every step of the way. I'll have your six."

"They can't know you're there," Liza said. "They killed the last assassin because he was sloppy. He didn't take out Liliana, and someone saw him make the attempt. He could've been identified and, if captured, he could've revealed information about the organization." She looked at the people on the big screen. "I have to prove the kill."

Dax and Liliana nodded.

"And you trust me to do it your way?"

"I do," Liliana said. "You escaped with your daughter once to keep from having to kill a stranger. I'm not a stranger anymore. If you couldn't kill a stranger, I doubt you can kill someone you know." She smiled. "Let's do this and get your daughter back."

Liza squared her shoulders and glanced down at the burner phone with the digital time displayed on the screen. "I have twenty-three hours and fourteen minutes to convince them I'm their assassin. Let's go."

CHAPTER 14

As promised, Utah had Liza's six all the way from Eagle Rock to West Yellowstone. The three-hour trip would take five, giving Liza enough time to pretend to case parking lots for the best car to steal or truck to hitch a ride with.

Sadie dressed Liza in black leather pants, a black long-sleeve top and a black leather jacket. She secured her hair in a tight coil at the nape of her neck and fit her with a black ski mask that covered everything but her eyes. To complete the outfit, Liza strapped the knife pouch she'd escaped with to her thigh.

Hank hooked her up with a radio headset and a tracking device.

Utah had the other radio, and he could use his cell phone to find Liza's tracker if he lost her at any point along the journey. Rather than trailing Liza in his truck, Utah had been given alternate transportation. Hank brought out a black BMW motorcycle, one of the quietest motorcycles Utah had ever driven. He'd been given a chance to practice driving it with Hank's instruction before leaving the ranch.

Though she'd wanted to leave immediately, Hank convinced Liza to wait a couple of hours before setting off. They needed time to let word leak out that Congresswoman Lightfeather would be moved from her safe house at two o'clock the following morning.

Delaying her start also gave Hank's people time to get ahead of her trek. They staged a car, a tractor-trailer rig and another car by the time Utah dropped Liza off outside of Eagle Rock.

She "stole" the first staged car parked next to a bar on the outskirts of Eagle Rock. She drove that car all the way through Bozeman to Four Corners, where she headed south on Highway 191. Utah followed, at a distance, lights out, on the back roads. Traveling through the towns, he kept closer without being right on her tail.

Liza ditched the stolen car a couple of blocks from a truck stop on the other side of Four Corners, located the staged tractor-trailer rig and stowed away in the trailer. The rig took her all the way to West Yellowstone, where it stopped at a truck stop for the night.

As planned, she "stole" the second car and drove

east out of West Yellowstone toward the safe house, arriving at the coordinates a little more than half a mile away from the house, tucked away in a wooded valley.

Utah followed, pulling off the road a mile short of Liza. From what Hank's team had reported, the watchers were within one hundred yards of the safe house. They were armed and would take out the congresswoman if given half a chance.

Earlier that evening before dark, a pizza delivery vehicle from West Yellowstone had made a delivery to the safe house.

Liliana had been stashed in the trunk of the little car and driven safely away. She was to have her picture taken at the morgue after having specialty makeup applied to make her appear as if she'd been shot in the head, with dried blood spattered across her face. In addition, she'd snipped a significant lock of hair and left it in the vehicle stored in the safe house's garage.

Not only did the pizza delivery driver bring pizza, he'd also brought a container of blood Hank's team had acquired from a local slaughterhouse. Dax would spread the blood throughout the car's interior before he drove it out of the garage. He and Liliana had created dummies by stuffing shirts and trousers with sheets and towels. They'd used pillowcases to form their heads. The dummies would be positioned inside the car before Dax drove away from the house.

After Utah parked his motorcycle, he hiked through the woods alongside the road until he was within twenty yards of Liza's GPS signal.

She arrived shortly after one in the morning and drove the car off the road into the brush, positioning it for a quick getaway. An AR-15 had been stashed under a blanket on the backseat floorboard.

She'd found it and sat behind the wheel, cradling the weapon in her lap, waiting for two o'clock for the show to begin.

"Hey," Utah spoke softly into his mic.

"Hey," she responded.

"You look badass with that AR-15 in your lap."

She looked around. "Where are you?"

"Your nine o'clock about twenty yards out."

Though she sat in the shadows, he could see her turn her head.

"I can't see you," she said.

"You're not supposed to. No one should see me."

She sighed. "It's nice to know you're there."

"I've been with you all the way."

"Thank you," she said. "It made it easier, knowing you had my back."

"Not much longer, and you'll be on your way to get Tayla," he said softly.

"Do you think they'll show up with her?" she asked, her voice so soft, he could barely hear her words.

"If they want their prized assassin, they will."

"Waiting sucks," she said.

He chuckled. "Yes. It does."

"Will Tayla and I ever be free of them?" Liza asked.

Utah wanted to tell her yes. But he'd be guessing. "Hank and Swede think the place where they are now has all the people from your compound and more. They think it's the main location and that the ones that've been shut down were satellite camps for specialized training. This location is in a canyon. From what they saw in the satellite images, there are several permanent structures situated near some rugged bluffs. The bluffs are dotted with caves. They've been studying the compound for several days via satellite. Trucks have been arriving full and leaving empty. They're stockpiling stuff."

"Great, they're getting ready to start a war, and my little girl is in the middle of all that."

"We don't know that," Utah said.

"I've never seen her happier than this morning... make that yesterday morning, when she was lying on the bed between us."

"She's a special person. So very easy to love. She's convinced me that children might not be as bad as I've thought all these years."

"Seriously? You don't like children?" Liza asked. "You could've fooled us."

"I grew up around adults. I didn't have any little friends to play with. The ones I met on rare occasions seemed so juvenile I didn't much care for them. I stayed away from other kids. Then I met you and Tayla. Now, I might even like kids. Who am I kidding?" Utah laughed. "Tayla had me wrapped around her little finger without even trying. I love that kid."

"Love?" Liza whispered.

Utah heard her. Had he really admitted to loving a child? "She's shown me it's okay to love someone even if you haven't known each other for very long. In fact," he said, going all in, "I'm well on my way to falling in love with Tayla's mother. Only, I'm afraid that by saying the L-word, I'll scare her off."

Silence stretched between them.

"See what I mean?" His voice shook. Why had he opened up so soon? Now it was out there, and she wasn't ready. He hadn't shown her how he could be good for her. How he would take care of her and Tayla. He hadn't proven himself worthy of them. Hell, he'd let the bad guys steal Tayla away on his watch.

"Oh, baby, I shouldn't have said anything."

"Did you mean it?" she asked.

"Yes," he said. "Every last word. I'm not just falling in love. I'm rip-my-heart-out-and-blow-me-away in love with a woman I don't deserve."

Again…silence.

Then softly, she said, "No man has ever said he loved me."

"I'm saying it now. When this charade is in the bag, I'll say it again." He glanced down at his watch. "Time to get in position. Keep your head low. We don't know what the watchers will do when the bullets start flying."

"You'll be here?"

"I promise," he said. "I've got our back."

"Here goes." Liza pushed open her door and slid out with her weapon, hunkering low. She had the ski mask pulled over her face. From what he could tell, she'd shed the black leather jacket. Moving from shadow to shadow, she eased up to the road, dropped to a prone position behind some scrub brush and waited.

Utah moved closer but still behind her, staying in the shadows. He couldn't risk being seen. He didn't trust the men TCW had sent to watch Liliana's and Liza's movements.

So far, everything had gone as planned. He hoped the rest of this exercise in deception went as smoothly.

LIZA LAY STILL, hoping to blend into the dirt, counting the seconds until this entire operation was over. Thankfully, she wasn't alone. Not only was Utah out there, but Hank's Yellowstone team had also been briefed and would move in as soon as the bullets started flying.

Now, all she had to do was wait for the car to arrive.

At two minutes past two o'clock, the rumble of an engine alerted her to the approaching car.

She sighted in on the road where the car would pass and lifted the barrel higher.

The car appeared in her peripheral vision.

She aimed above the roof and fired.

The car swerved slightly, slowed and the driver's door opened. A man dove out, kicking the door closed behind him. The car continued to roll down the road.

With the driver lying low in the ditch, Liza peppered the vehicle with bullets as it rolled like a slow automaton. Eventually, it veered off the road and hit a tree.

Liza scrambled to her feet. Carrying the AR-15, she ran across the road, into the ditch on the other side and pulled open the back door.

When the car had gone off the road and smacked into the tree, everything in the back seat slid onto the floor. Including the black hair that should have been on the seat within easy reach,

Liza had to climb over the dummy in the back seat, shift its legs and feel around on the floor for the clump of hair and the necklace Lilianna had promised would be there. Unwilling to use a flashlight, Liza wasted too many seconds searching, but she couldn't give up. Everything hinged on the proof she needed to show to Spike.

Her fingers slid across something soft.

The hair lay in a clump, secured with a rubber band.

Patting the floor close to the hair, Liza located the necklace. Her proof in hand, she stuffed the items into her pocket, backed off the seat and slipped out of the vehicle.

Shots rang out, and bullets pinged against metal near Liza's head.

She dove to the ground with the AR-15 in her hands. Though she'd used a lot of the rounds in the magazine, she was certain she hadn't used all thirty.

"Liza?" Utah's voice sounded in her ear.

"Still among the living."

"That wasn't you firing, was it?"

"No."

"Didn't think so. Stay down."

"Will do," she answered and low-crawled away from the car until she reached the stand of brush she'd hidden behind when she'd fired on the vehicle.

More shots rang out. This time in rapid succession, like war had broken out.

Liza studied the darkness, unable to pinpoint the source. She didn't want to return fire, especially when she couldn't see who was doing the firing. It could be the watchers. Or maybe Hank's Yellowstone team. Not knowing where anyone was, Liza lay low.

Until they ran out of bullets, or their weapons jammed, she wasn't going anywhere.

Moments later, silence descended on the crashed vehicle in the ditch.

Liza crawled through the dirt, brush and brambles, staying as close to the ground as possible. When she was far enough away from the crashed vehicle, she rose and ran for the car she'd parked in the brush.

Once there, she dove into the driver's seat and cranked the engine. Shoving the shift into drive, she hit the accelerator hard. The little car leaped out of the bushes and up onto the road.

Bullets pinged against the exterior. One pierced the windshield just above Liza's head. If she'd only learned one thing from her daring escape from the compound, it was to stay low and don't stop. She sank lower and kept driving.

"You there?" she said into her mic.

"I am. Holding back to make sure no one follows you."

Determined to put as much distance between her and whoever was shooting at her, she didn't stop until she'd blown through West Yellowstone. On the other side of town, she looked down at the burner phone. Reception was down to two bars. If she wanted to make that call, it had to be before she got too far outside town.

She checked her rearview mirror. If Utah was back there, she couldn't see him.

Liza turned over the cell phone and memorized the number. She entered the digits, pushed aside her headset and pressed the cell phone to her ear. As she waited, her breath lodged in her throat and a knot formed in her chest.

"You got the proof?" Spike's voice boomed in her ear.

"I do," was her breathless response.

"Head to Bozeman. When you're back in cell phone reception, call for your next instructions."

"Wait," Liza said. "I want proof of life, or I'm not coming."

"Getting a little sassy?" Spike asked.

"I want proof my daughter is alive and well."

"You'd have me wake her?" Spike snorted. "What kind of mother are you?"

"One who cares," she answered. "I want to hear her voice."

A few moments later, Tayla's groggy voice filled Liza's ear. "Mommy?"

The sound of her daughter's voice brought tears to Liza's eyes. "Hey, baby."

"You got your proof. Now, get to Bozeman." Spike ended the call.

"Did you make the call?" Utah asked in her headset.

She slid it over her ear. "I did. About to call Swede to see if he was able to locate the source."

"Do it." Utah went silent.

Liza dialed the number Swede had given her.

He answered on the first ring, "Got the coordinates," he answered. "Hank and a couple of others are heading that way."

"Is it time to call in the law?" she asked.

"Not if you want to see your daughter again," Swede warned. "These people have backup plans for their backup plans. It's why they're so hard to find."

"Don't let them get away with my daughter," Liza whispered.

"We'll do the best we can," Swede said.

Liza ended the call.

"Utah?" she said.

"Yeah, babe?" he answered immediately.

"I'm headed to Bozeman for my next instructions."

"I'll be back here if you need someone to talk to."

Liza smiled. It was nice to have someone watching her back. Especially if that someone was handsome, kind to animals and children and made her body sing.

She pressed the accelerator to the floor. Despite going over ninety miles per hour, the drive back seemed to take forever.

As soon as she got service, she called Swede first. "Did they make it to his location?" she asked.

"I'm sorry to say our guy went to the coordinates, and they'd moved on."

"Damn!" Liza's hopes were taking a beating. "I'm about to call him again. Be ready."

"On it," Swede said.

Liza punched in the numbers.

"Took you long enough," Spike grumbled.

"Where's my daughter?" Liza demanded.

"In good hands," he said. "In good hands."

"Bullshit," Liza cried. "I did what you asked. I have proof. I want my daughter."

"Meet me in Diablo Canyon at the overlook in twenty minutes. If you're not there in twenty, we're done, and Tayla is ours for good."

"Understand this," Liza said, her tone tight, "Tayla will never be yours. I'll be there in fifteen."

She'd continued driving and was already on the other side of Bozeman, heading toward Eagle Rock.

Diablo Canyon was between Bozeman and Eagle Rock on back roads that twisted between hills and valleys. The canyon had been carved out by glaciers thousands of years before.

Before she left good cell phone reception, she called Swede.

"We got his location and have men on their way," Swede said. "He's out near Diablo Canyon."

"That's where he said we'll meet," she said.

"Our guys will be there in fifteen minutes."

"Make it ten," she said and ended the call. "Utah, you still there?"

"I am," he responded.

"I'm meeting Spike in Diablo Canyon."

"Let Hank's guys get ahead of you," Utah said. "We need them in place before any shit hits the fan."

"He has my daughter. I can't wait."

Utah muttered a curse. "Do me a favor."

"What favor?" she asked.

"Don't get yourself shot."

"I'll do my best," she promised.

"Okay," Utah said. "Let's go get our girl."

Her heart warmed at his words as it pushed adrenaline through her veins.

She was going to get her daughter. The bastards holding her had better not get in her way.

CHAPTER 15

UTAH COULDN'T LET Liza drive straight into the lion's den. The closer they got to the canyon turnoff, the more worried he became.

"Hey, babe," he called out over the radio.

"Hey," she answered.

"How far past the turn-off is the overlook?" he asked.

"I don't know," she said. "Maybe half a mile. It's been years since we came here as teens."

"Pull off the road a mile before the turn-off," he said.

"Why?"

"Humor me," he said. "I have an idea."

"I want to get to Tayla," she insisted.

"I don't want you to walk right into their trap."

She hesitated. "Okay."

A mile before the turn-off, Liza pulled the car off

the road and parked behind a stand of trees and brush.

Utah slowed the motorcycle and pulled in behind her. He got off the bike and crossed to where she sat behind the wheel.

"My baby is so close I can hardly stand to wait for another second," she said.

"You know they're going to use her to bring you back into their fold."

"Or lure me out so they can shoot me." She huffed out a breath. "What else can I do? I have to show up."

"Be there, but don't give them something to shoot at or grab."

Her brow furrowed in the light from the stars above. "I don't understand."

"Let me have the rifle."

She reached under the blanket on the back floorboard and handed him the AR-15. "I'm not sure how many rounds are left in the magazine."

He released the magazine. "Enough to make a statement," he said, shoving the magazine back into the weapon. "Come on. We're going in on foot."

Her brow furrowed. "It's over a mile in. That'll take longer than I told them I'd be."

"Not if we hurry and cut through the woods." He opened her car door and held it while she climbed out.

"They'll have guards posted, watching for us," she warned.

"Then we'll have to find them first," Utah said. "This way, we get a chance to check them out before you let them know you're there." He pulled her into his arms and kissed her. "We're going to get her back."

Liza nodded. "Let's go."

Utah led the way, using the compass on his watch to navigate through the woods, heading directly for the overlook. He'd checked the position on the map and aimed in that general direction.

After several minutes of climbing over fallen trees or pushing aside the branches of trees, Utah sensed they were getting close. He stopped in the shadow of a tree and stared through the woods, searching for movement.

A moment later, he saw something move near the road leading into the canyon.

Leaning with his back against a tree, a man sat on the ground with a rifle resting in his lap.

Utah motioned for Liza to get down and stay put.

He slipped into the woods, treading soundlessly.

The man on the ground never knew what hit him. Utah came at him from behind, got him in a choke hold and held on until the man passed out. Then he pulled zip-ties from his pocket and secured the man's wrists and ankles. Afraid he'd wake and raise a ruckus, Utah pulled off his boot and sock and stuffed the sock into the man's mouth.

He hurried back for Liza, and they continued toward the overlook.

As they neared the clearing, Utah counted six men he could see. He'd bet there were at least three more hidden in the woods. At least they were down one on the road.

Utah leaned close to Liza's ear. "We need to stall until Hank's men get here."

She nodded. "I'm going in."

He caught her arm. "Talk. Don't show them where you are at first. It'll put them off balance."

Liza stepped closer to the clearing around the overlook and blended into the shadows.

Utah knelt beside another tree and raised the rifle to his shoulder, ready to take down anyone who even looked like he wanted to hurt Liza or Tayla.

"I'm here," Liza called out. "Where's my daughter?"

The men spun, holding handguns out in front of them.

Spike stepped out of an SUV and frowned. "Where are you? Show yourself."

"Not until you show me my daughter," she replied.

Spike reached into the SUV and dragged Tayla out by her arm.

Her daughter tugged hard, trying to get loose. When that didn't work, she kicked Spike in the shin.

"Damn brat!" He yanked her up into his arms and

held her tightly against him. "Here's your spawn. Show me the proof."

"Didn't your people watching me give you an update? Or were they too busy trying to kill me?"

"At least they know how to follow orders." Spike held out his hand. "Give me the proof, or I leave with the kid."

Liza wrapped the hair and the necklace together with the rubber band. Using the necklace chain like a lasso, she twirled it around her finger and let it fly across the clearing to land at Spike's feet.

All eyes turned in her direction. She refused to step out into the open. The longer they wondered where she was, the more time Hank's men had to get there.

"Mommy?"

"I'm here, baby," she answered.

Spike bent to retrieve the hair and necklace. After a moment, he tossed them to the ground. "These items prove nothing."

"Then have your guys check out the morgue," Liza said. "The target and the driver will be there with all the proof you need. Or if you don't want to wait, call the M.E. He'll tell you."

Spike glared. "You're not getting the kid until I get confirmation that she's dead."

"Give me my daughter," Liza said through clenched teeth.

"We're done here," Spike turned with Tayla in his arms and started to climb into the SUV.

Her heart racing and out of options, Liza yelled. "Stop!"

"Guess you'll have to make me," Spike said.

Liza's hands dropped to her sides. How would she force Spike to give Tayla back?

She couldn't let him get into the SUV with her daughter.

Her fingers brushed across the pouch of throwing knives and lifted one out automatically. The cool steel felt natural in her hand. She'd thrown from this distance before with excellent accuracy. Could she hit a moving target…one that held her daughter in his arms?

It was do something or lose her daughter forever.

Liza raised her arm, aiming at Spike.

Breathe in, breathe out…and hold.

She let the knife fly. It hit Spike where she'd aimed…in the neck.

The bald man screamed, dropped Tayla, grabbed the knife and pulled it free.

Tayla landed on her feet and took off running for the woods.

Blood gushed from the wound, drenching Spike's neck, shoulders and the front of his shirt.

"Bitch!" he screamed, clamping a hand over the wound in an attempt to stem the flow. "Get her, damn it!"

Men ran toward her. They might not see her yet, but they would if they got too much closer.

Liza couldn't follow Tayla, or she'd give up her position. When they found her, it would be all over. She prayed Tayla didn't get lost and fall over a cliff.

She pulled another knife from the pouch.

As a man neared, she slowly cocked her arm.

"Any one of you take another step, and I'll shoot," Utah called out from his position in the shadows.

"You let her get away, and I'll shoot you myself." Spike ran toward them, roaring like an angry lion. "That bitch must pay."

The men ran for the woods, more afraid of Spike than a stranger in the shadows.

A shot rang out, and one of the men dropped to the ground.

The others kept coming.

Liza aimed and let the knife fly. It hit the man closest to her square in the chest. He staggered several steps, then fell to his knees.

Utah fired another shot and nailed a guy ten feet from where Liza stood.

Her heart skittered and thundered against her ribs. Another man came at her.

Before she could reach for another knife, he was on her.

She went into defensive mode, deflected his advance and sent him stumbling headfirst into a tree. He dropped to his knees.

With his men falling one by one, Spike ran for the SUV, still holding tightly to his neck.

Liza went after him. She couldn't let him get away.

"Liza!" Utah called out behind her. "Get down! Now!"

Liza hit the ground.

A shot rang out.

Spike jerked, staggered several more feet, fell into the SUV then slid to the ground.

Headlights shone on the road leading to the overlook. Men dropped down out of the trucks and SUVs and ran the stragglers to the ground.

Liza ran in the direction Tayla had gone. "Tayla, baby, it's okay. You can come out now."

When she didn't respond, Liza's heart leaped into her throat. They were so close to the canyon's edge. "Tayla! Please. Come out. Everything's going to be all right."

"Tayla," Utah joined Liza. "The good guys are here now. You can come out of hiding."

Rustling among the trees sent Utah and Liza rushing toward the sound.

They skidded to a stop when a man stepped out of the shadows, holding Tayla with his hand over her mouth and a gun to her head. "One step closer, and the kid gets it."

"Let her go," Liza said.

"Put down your gun, man," Utah said. "It's over. Your people are either dead or captured."

"I'm getting out alive, and this kid is my ticket out." He lifted his chin. "Step aside. I have nothing left to lose, so don't test me."

Tayla squirmed in the man's arms.

"Be still, you miserable brat." He fought to hold her and the gun.

Tayla's eyes narrowed. Then she bit the man's hand clamped over her mouth.

The man yelled, dropped Tayla and swung the gun toward Liza.

She had a knife out and thrown as the man pulled the trigger.

The bullet nicked her shoulder, sending a brief stab of pain through her arm.

Her knife hit pay dirt and lodged in the man's throat. He dropped the gun, clutched the knife and pulled it free. When he started toward her, Utah fired.

The man fell to the ground.

Tayla ran to Liza and launched herself into her arms.

Liza winced and gritted her teeth. The pain was worth it. She had her daughter back in her arms.

Utah wrapped his arms around both of them and held them close. When he realized Liza was bleeding on them, he stepped back.

"Let's get you to a doctor."

She laughed. "Why? It's just a flesh wound."

"I don't care. It can get infected." He took Tayla from her arms and herded them toward the men who'd come to clean up what was left of Spike's gang.

He was surprised to find his teammates were the men Hank had sent.

Drake settled Tayla in an SUV while Utah buckled Liza in.

"What happened to Hank and his crew?" Liza asked.

"He tapped all of his guys to raid the camp they found. The sheriff's department and FBI are there as well." Drake's lips twisted. "Hank can pull some strings when he sets his mind to it. I'm thinking of joining him when our gig is up at the Lucky Lady."

Utah nodded. "I'm leaning in that direction, too. But right now, we need to get these ladies to a doctor and then out to Hank's house. We promised Tayla she could play with Emma."

"Skip the doctor. I want to get out to Hank's and find out what's going on," Liza said.

Drake looked from Liza to Utah. "Grimm, Judge, and Murdock can stay and answer questions when the sheriff's deputies arrive. By the way, they're on the way. And Liza's right, Swede will know something."

Utah frowned. "Okay, but if that flesh wound needs stitches, we're going back to town to get them."

Liza grinned. "Deal. Now, shut up and get in."

Utah handed her a handful of tissues to hold against her wound.

She might be wounded, but her life was looking up. She had Tayla, Utah loved her and her nemesis, Spike, was dead. Good riddance to the bastard. She couldn't find it in her heart to feel bad about killing him. He'd threatened Tayla once too often.

She wasn't out of danger yet, but Spike had been the main force behind putting her to work as an assassin. With him gone, maybe the others wouldn't think twice about her.

Hopefully, Hank and his task force would gather up the others before they scattered to the winds. She prayed PJ was one of the recruits rescued.

CHAPTER 16

Before they left the canyon lookout, Utah arranged for Murdock and Grimm to bring the motorcycle and "stolen" car back to Hank's place.

Drake drove Utah, Liza and Tayla to White Oak Ranch, where Sadie greeted them with hugs and a first aid kit. She had Liza's "flesh wound" cleaned, disinfected and bandaged in short order. The movie star wasn't afraid of blood or getting her hands dirty.

"I'm married to Hank Patterson." She laughed. "I don't have time to be squeamish." Her gaze went to the little girls playing on the living room floor and her son McClain, doing his best to crawl into the middle of their fun. "And there are the children." She smiled at Utah and Liza. "I have the best life."

Swede manned the communications base in the basement, answering calls from the Yellowstone, Colorado and Eagle Rock Protectors, taking clients' calls and monitoring the police scanner. When he had downtime, he continued his review of satellite images in his search for other compounds they might have missed.

Liza wore a path on the stairs in and out of the basement, eager for news of the raid and punchy about leaving Tayla alone for any length of time.

Every time she got within two feet of Utah, he wrapped her in his arms, held her for a few seconds then let go. She liked it. Maybe too much. She was getting used to having him around and so was Tayla.

At one point, Liza had come up from the basement to find Utah on the floor of the living room with a tiara on his head, reading a story to the children about a princess and a prince who fell in love but had to fight the evil bad guy to get their happily ever after.

When the story was over, Tayla's brow wrinkled. She looked up at Utah. "Are you the prince, and is Mommy the princess?" She shot a glance at Liza. "You fought the evil bad guy and won. Does that mean you get to have a happy-ever-after?"

Liza couldn't burst her joyful bubble and tell her they would probably have to hide again if the bad guys came after them. Instead, she smiled. "Yes, ma'am. It's happily-ever-after for the good guys."

Emma clapped her hands. "My daddy is a good guy. He's a prince."

"My daddy is a good guy, too." Tayla's eyes widened. "I mean, my Utah is a good guy, too."

Liza's heart pinched hard in her chest. Tayla was a usually happy little girl, no matter the crappy circumstances. However, she was beginning to realize she didn't have a daddy. Emma had one. Why couldn't she?

Utah, with his princess crown on his head, would make a wonderful father for Tayla and any other children that might come along.

Liza spun away, afraid Utah might read her thoughts. Which was ridiculous. But if he could, would he run screaming from the room, feeling trapped by a woman who came as part of a package deal?

Hadn't he professed his love for her and her daughter? Had he really meant it?

A bright shaft of joy wedged its way into Liza's cautious heart. Could they stay in Eagle Rock and make a life together?

A lot depended on what was happening at the TCW compound raid.

Even Swede hadn't heard much. He'd gleaned what he could from the police scanner.

LATE THAT EVENING, Hank reported in. "We're on our way back. We'll have a debrief in the war room before everyone goes their own way."

Murdock, Grimm, Drake and Judge arrived well before Hank and his team. After Drake had dropped off Utah, Liza and Tayla, he'd gone back out to help the overloaded sheriff's department and coroner wrangle Spike's minions and process the dead.

Utah met them with cold beers on the porch. "What a day."

"Tell me about it," Murdock said. "This was not how I pictured my honeymoon."

"That's right. You're supposed to be on your honeymoon."

"I'm lucky that my wife, the veterinarian, understands emergency house calls and prioritizing family at the top of the list." He grinned. "We've postponed the honeymoon another month. She's got a sick horse she doesn't want to leave."

"The sheriff will send someone by tomorrow to get your statements," Drake informed Utah and Liza. "We might have to do it again if the FBI wants to weigh in."

An hour later, after the sun had dropped below the mountain peaks, Hank and his guys trudged up the porch stairs and followed him into the basement.

Sadie, Utah and Liza were ready with a huge tray of sandwiches, an ice chest of cold beer and sodas.

The men gladly grabbed the first food they'd had all day and sat around the table.

For the next forty-five minutes, they discussed

the operation, what they'd found and what they hadn't found.

"It was the main compound," Hank said. "We found people who'd been at the other two compounds who'd been moved when their locations had been compromised."

He met Liza's gaze. "One of the leaders we captured went by the name Commander."

Liza let go of the breath she'd been holding. "Good." Without Spike and Commander calling the shots for the people who'd been under their training command, Liza dared to hope she could live a normal life.

"Did you find a woman called PJ?" Liza asked.

Hank shook his head. "We looked and questioned everyone who was rounded up, and no one answered to PJ or knew anyone with those initials."

"Then you didn't get everyone." Liza would like to have helped PJ escape TCW. As long as Swede and Hank kept looking, there was hope.

"We rounded up a lot of their leaders, but we think we haven't successfully captured their number one man in charge."

"Until then, we should all be on our toes and look out for each other." Hank looked around the room. "Thank you all for the effort today. You're amazing, and I appreciate everything you do as Brotherhood Protectors." He smiled at Utah and the other men of his remodeling team. "And thank you to Team Lucky

Lady. We called, and you answered. I consider you five honorary Brotherhood Protectors. The door's always open when you decide to accept the job for real."

He clapped his hands together. "If that's everything, get some rest. Good job!"

The men pushed away from the table and climbed the stairs. Some stood around talking, but most left to go home.

Sadie showed Liza and Utah to their rooms across the hall from one another.

Liza settled Tayla in bed and then crossed the hall. She had just raised her hand to knock on Utah's door when it opened.

He grabbed her hand, pulled her into his arms and crushed her to his chest. "How is it we've been in the same house most of the day...a house full of people...and I missed you?"

She rested her cheek against his chest. "I know what you mean. I miss this." She snuggled closer and wrapped her arms around his waist. "Did you mean what you said about loving Tayla and me?"

"Every word. It scares me and makes me happy at the same time. Believe it or not, I've never been in love before. I wasn't even sure this ache in my chest was love. I thought maybe it was a heart attack or heartburn, something I'd die from or get over soon. I haven't died, and there's no getting over the way I feel." He brushed his lips across hers in a kiss so gentle it left her wanting more. "It has to be love. And if it takes a lifetime for you to fall in love with me, I'll wait. Because you and Tayla are worth it."

She shook her head. "I'm afraid to love. Afraid the organization will continue to haunt us, to come after Tayla and me. How can I expect someone to live with that kind of fear?"

"Give me the choice," he said. "I know it's all new, and we haven't known each other long, but do you think you could love me someday?"

"Are you serious?" Liza shook her head. "I fell in love with you when you pulled me off the side of that cliff and saved Tayla and me. I fell even deeper when you wore that silly tiara and read fairytales to the kids this afternoon. I knew I should keep running, to disappear so they couldn't find us, but I couldn't leave you. I love you, Pierce Turner, and if there is a happily-ever-after for me, it can only happen because you are part of my story."

She kissed her prince and followed him into his room to show him just how much she loved him and wanted him to be a part of her and Tayla's story.

EPILOGUE

Two weeks later

"Liza, Tayla!" Utah backed through the cottage door, balancing a box in his hand. A grin had ruled his face from the time he'd gotten in his truck in Eagle Rock to when he'd arrived at their temporary home on the White Oak Ranch.

"Liza, Tayla! Where are you? I have something you're going to want to see." He moved through the little house, checking the kitchen, the living room, Tayla's bedroom decorated in an explosion of colors, sunlight pouring through the window, and no Tayla.

His brow furrowing, Utah continued to the back of the house, passing the master bedroom he shared with Liza and the laundry room.

His heart beat faster. Where were they? A flashback of the abduction in front of the Lucky Lady Lodge hit him square in the gut. Had the TCW found their way through Hank Patterson's security and snatched the two women Utah loved most out from under his nose?

He burst through the back door, his gaze panning the yard with the white picket fence and a swing set he'd erected the past weekend with Liza and Tayla's assistance.

"Liza! Tayla! Sweet Jesus, where are you?"

Liza ran around the side of the house, her eyes round, gardening gloves covered in soil, and dirt on the knees of her jeans. "What's wrong? Is the house on fire? The plumbing spring another leak? Why are you yelling?"

Utah sucked in a deep breath and let it out slowly, releasing the tension with it. "I got a little worried when I couldn't find you." He looked over her shoulder. "Where's Tayla?"

"She's helping me plant onions and carrots. Are you all right?" Her gaze swept over the box he carried.

"Never better," he said. "Tayla! Come here. I have something you'll want to see." He set the box on the ground.

"What's in the box?" Liza asked, moving closer.

"I'll show you as soon as Tayla gets over here. Tayla!"

The three-year-old ran around the side of the house, her hand covered in dirt up to her elbows and a big smudge across her right cheek. "What's in the box, Daddy Utah?"

"Now that you're here, open it, so you and your mama can see.

With happy excitement, Tayla rushed to the box and reached for the flaps.

The box lurched. Something made a scratching sound inside.

Tayla jerked her hand back, her gaze going to Utah.

"It's okay. It won't hurt you." Utah waved toward the box. "Go on, open it."

A bit more tentatively, she pulled one of the flaps over, then another and looked inside.

Tayla screamed with joy, clapped her hands over her cheeks and burst into tears.

Liza shook her head. "What the devil's in the box?"

Utah reached into the box and scooped up a wiggling, licking, ball of canine cuddles. "Do you want to hold her?" Utah went down on his haunches and held out the golden retriever puppy.

Tayla wiped her tears and held out her arms.

Utah laid the puppy in her little arms and wrapped them around the animal. "You have to be careful not to squeeze her too hard. She's just a baby and needs lots of tender loving care."

Tayla looked up at Utah, more tears swimming in her eyes. "Is it for me? My own puppy?" More tears slipped down her cheeks.

Utah nodded, appalled that what he'd been sure she would like had made his sunny little girl cry so hard. "I thought you'd like a puppy. Is she not the right kind? Do you want me to take her back?"

"No," Tayla wailed, hugging the puppy close. "She's perfect. I love her so much." More tears fell.

Utah turned to Liza. "What did I do wrong?"

Liza had tears in her eyes as well. She sniffed and brushed them from her cheeks. "You did nothing wrong and everything right." She flung her arms around his neck and hugged him tight. Now, tears soaked his T-shirt.

"I'm having a really hard time understanding girls today."

Liza laughed and scrubbed the moisture from her cheeks. "You'll never understand women, babe."

"So, let me get this straight." He pointed at the puppy. "You like the puppy? But you're crying." He shook his head. "I don't get it."

Tayla nodded, burying her face in the puppy's soft fur. "Thank you, Daddy Utah. Thank you. I love her so much, and I'm going to call her Daisy."

Liza gave Utah a watery smile. "Those are happy tears. You just made Tayla the happiest little girl ever. And you've made me the happiest big girl ever. I love you so very much."

Utah pulled his girls into his arms, tears, puppy and all. He'd never understand them, but he loved them to the moon and back.

BREAKING SILENCE

DELTA FORCE STRONG BOOK #1

New York Times & USA Today
Bestselling Author

ELLE JAMES

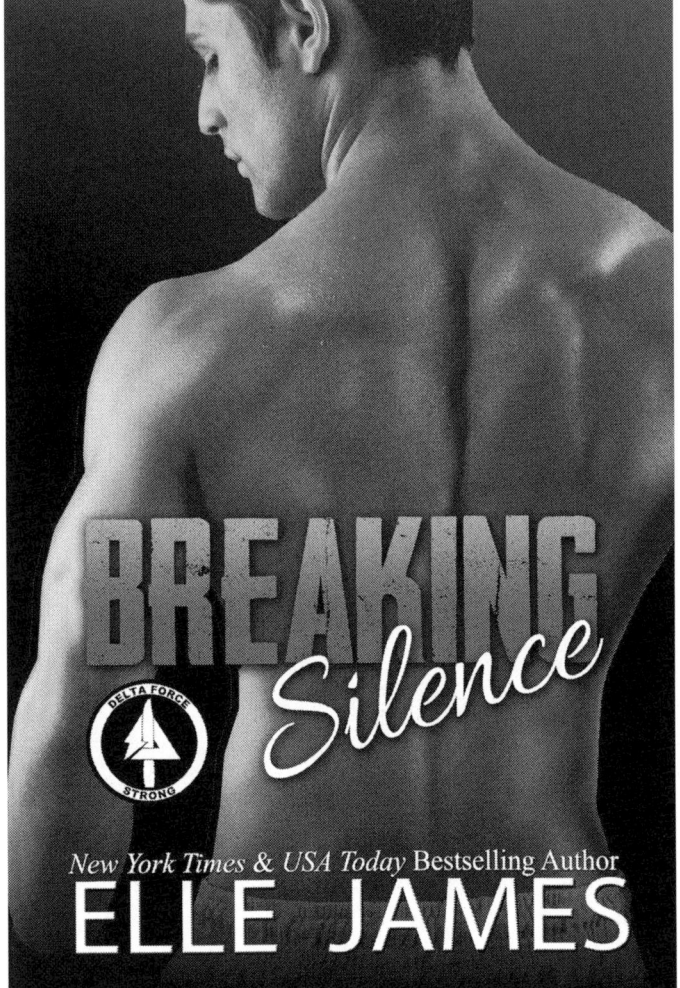

CHAPTER 1

HAD he known they would be deployed so soon after their last short mission to El Salvador, Rucker Sloan wouldn't have bought that dirt bike from his friend Duff. Now, it would sit there for months before he actually got to take it out to the track.

The team had been given forty-eight hours to pack their shit, take care of business and get onto the C130 that would transport them to Afghanistan.

Now, boots on the ground, duffel bags stowed in their assigned quarters behind the wire, they were ready to take on any mission the powers that be saw fit to assign.

What he wanted most that morning, after being awake for the past thirty-six hours, was a cup of strong, black coffee.

The rest of his team had hit the sack as soon as

they got in. Rucker had already met with their commanding officer, gotten a brief introduction to the regional issues and had been told to get some rest. They'd be operational within the next forty-eight hours.

Too wound up to sleep, Rucker followed a stream of people he hoped were heading for the chow hall. He should be able to get coffee there.

On the way, he passed a sand volleyball court where two teams played against each other. One of the teams had four players, the other only three. The four-person squad slammed a ball to the ground on the other side of the net. The only female player ran after it as it rolled toward Rucker.

He stopped the ball with his foot and picked it up.

The woman was tall, slender, blond-haired and blue-eyed. She wore an Army PT uniform of shorts and an Army T-shirt with her hair secured back from her face in a ponytail seated on the crown of her head.

Without makeup, and sporting a sheen of perspiration, she was sexy as hell, and the men on both teams knew it.

They groaned when Rucker handed her the ball. He'd robbed them of watching the female soldier bending over to retrieve the runaway.

She took the ball and frowned. "Do you play?"

"I have," he answered.

"We could use a fourth." She lifted her chin in challenge.

Tired from being awake for the past thirty-six hours, Rucker opened his mouth to say *hell no*. But he made the mistake of looking into her sky-blue eyes and instead said, "I'm in."

What the hell was he thinking?

Well, hadn't he been wound up from too many hours sitting in transit? What he needed was a little physical activity to relax his mind and muscles. At least, that's what he told himself in the split-second it took to step into the sandbox and serve up a heaping helping of whoop-ass.

He served six times before the team playing opposite finally returned one. In between each serve, his side gave him high-fives, all members except one—the blonde with the blue eyes he stood behind, admiring the length of her legs beneath her black Army PT shorts.

Twenty minutes later, Rucker's team won the match. The teams broke up and scattered to get showers or breakfast in the chow hall.

"Can I buy you a cup of coffee?" the pretty blonde asked.

"Only if you tell me your name." He twisted his lips into a wry grin. "I'd like to know who delivered those wicked spikes."

She held out her hand. "Nora Michaels," she said.

He gripped her hand in his, pleased to feel firm pressure. Women might be the weaker sex, but he didn't like a dead fish handshake from males or females. Firm and confident was what he preferred. Like her ass in those shorts.

She cocked an eyebrow. "And you are?"

He'd been so intent thinking about her legs and ass, he'd forgotten to introduce himself. "Rucker Sloan. Just got in less than an hour ago."

"Then you could probably use a tour guide to the nearest coffee."

He nodded. "Running on fumes here. Good coffee will help."

"I don't know about good, but it's coffee and it's fresh." She released his hand and fell in step beside him, heading in the direction of some of the others from their volleyball game.

"As long as it's strong and black, I'll be happy."

She laughed. "And awake for the next twenty-four hours."

"Spoken from experience?" he asked, casting a glance in her direction.

She nodded. "I work nights in the medical facility. It can be really boring and hard to stay awake when we don't have any patients to look after." She held up her hands. "Not that I want any of our boys injured and in need of our care."

"But it does get boring," he guessed.

"It makes for a long deployment." She held out her

hand. "Nice to meet you, Rucker. Is Rucker a call sign or your real name?"

He grinned. "Real name. That was the only thing my father gave me before he cut out and left my mother and me to make it on our own."

"Your mother raised you, and you still joined the Army?" She raised an eyebrow. "Most mothers don't want their boys to go off to war."

"It was that or join a gang and end up dead in a gutter," he said. "She couldn't afford to send me to college. I was headed down the gang path when she gave me the ultimatum. Join and get the GI-Bill, or she would cut me off and I'd be out in the streets. To her, it was the only way to get me out of L.A. and to have the potential to go to college someday."

She smiled "And you stayed in the military."

He nodded. "I found a brotherhood that was better than any gang membership in LA. For now, I take college classes online. It was my mother's dream for me to graduate college. She never went, and she wanted so much more for me than the streets of L.A.. When my gig is up with the Army, if I haven't finished my degree, I'll go to college fulltime."

"And major in what?" Nora asked.

"Business management. I'm going to own my own security service. I want to put my combat skills to use helping people who need dedicated and specialized protection."

Nora nodded. "Sounds like a good plan."

"I know the protection side of things. I need to learn the business side and business law. Life will be different on the civilian side."

"True."

"How about you? What made you sign up?" he asked.

She shrugged. "I wanted to put my nursing degree to good use and help our men and women in uniform. This is my first assignment after training."

"Drinking from the firehose?" Rucker stopped in front of the door to the mess hall.

She nodded. "Yes. But it's the best baptism under fire medical personnel can get. I'll be a better nurse for it when I return to the States."

"How much longer do you have to go?" he asked, hoping that she'd say she'd be there as long as he was. In his case, he never knew how long their deployments would last. One week, one month, six months…

She gave him a lopsided smile. "I ship out in a week."

"That's too bad." He opened the door for her. "I just got here. That doesn't give us much time to get to know each other."

"That's just as well." Nora stepped through the door. "I don't want to be accused of fraternizing. I'm too close to going back to spoil my record."

Rucker chuckled. "Playing volleyball and sharing a table while drinking coffee won't get you written up. I like the way you play. I'm curious to know where you learned to spike like that."

"I guess that's reasonable. Coffee first." She led him into the chow hall.

The smells of food and coffee made Rucker's mouth water.

He grabbed a tray and loaded his plate with eggs, toast and pancakes drenched in syrup. Last, he stopped at the coffee urn and filled his cup with freshly brewed black coffee.

When he looked around, he found Nora seated at one of the tables, holding a mug in her hands, a small plate with cottage cheese and peaches on it.

He strode over to her. "Mind if I join you?"

"As long as you don't hit on me," she said with cocked eyebrows.

"You say that as if you've been hit on before."

She nodded and sipped her steaming brew. "I lost count how many times in the first week I was here."

"Shows they have good taste in women and, unfortunately, limited manners."

"And you're better?" she asked, a smile twitching the corners of her lips.

"I'm not hitting on you. You can tell me to leave, and I'll be out of this chair so fast, you won't have time to enunciate the V."

She stared straight into his eyes, canted her head to one side and said, "Leave."

In the middle of cutting into one of his pancakes,

Rucker dropped his knife and fork on the tray, shot out of his chair and left with his tray, sloshing coffee as he moved. He hoped she was just testing him. If she wasn't…oh, well. He was used to eating meals alone. If she was, she'd have to come to him.

He took a seat at the next table, his back to her, and resumed cutting into his pancake.

Nora didn't utter a word behind him.

Oh, well. He popped a bite of syrupy sweet pancake in his mouth and chewed thoughtfully. She was only there for another week. Man, she had a nice ass…and those legs… He sighed and bent over his plate to stab his fork into a sausage link.

"This chair taken?" a soft, female voice sounded in front of him.

He looked up to see the pretty blond nurse standing there with her tray in her hands, a crooked smile on her face.

He lifted his chin in silent acknowledgement.

She laid her tray on the table and settled onto the chair. "I didn't think you'd do it."

"Fair enough. You don't know me," he said.

"I know that you joined the Army to get out of street life. That your mother raised you after your father skipped out, that you're working toward a business degree and that your name is Rucker." She sipped her coffee.

He nodded, secretly pleased she'd remembered all

that. Maybe there was hope for getting to know the pretty nurse before she redeployed to the States. And who knew? They might run into each other on the other side of the pond.

Still, he couldn't show too much interest, or he'd be no better than the other guys who'd hit on her. "Since you're redeploying back to the States in a week, and I'm due to go out on a mission, probably within the next twenty-four to forty-eight hours, I don't know if it's worth our time to get to know each other any more than we already have."

She nodded. "I guess that's why I want to sit with you. You're not a danger to my perfect record of no fraternizing. I don't have to worry that you'll fall in love with me in such a short amount of time." She winked.

He chuckled. "As I'm sure half of this base has fallen in love with you since you've been here."

She shrugged. "I don't know if it's love, but it's damned annoying."

"How so?"

She rolled her eyes toward the ceiling. "I get flowers left on my door every day."

"And that's annoying? I'm sure it's not easy coming up with flowers out here in the desert." He set down his fork and took up his coffee mug. "I think it's sweet." He held back a smile. Well, almost.

"They're hand-drawn on notepad paper and left

on the door of my quarters and on the door to the shower tent." She shook her head. "It's kind of creepy and stalkerish."

Rucker nodded. "I see your point. The guys should at least have tried their hands at origami flowers, since the real things are scarce around here."

Nora smiled. "I'm not worried about the pictures, but the line for sick call is ridiculous."

"How so?"

"So many of the guys come up with the lamest excuses to come in and hit on me. I asked to work the nightshift to avoid sick call altogether."

"You have a fan group." He smiled. "Has the adoration gone to your head?"

She snorted softly. "No."

"You didn't get this kind of reaction back in the States?"

"I haven't been on active duty for long. I only decided to join the Army after my mother passed away. I was her fulltime nurse for a couple years as she went through stage four breast cancer. We thought she might make it." Her shoulders sagged. "But she didn't."

"I'm sorry to hear that. My mother meant a lot to me, as well. I sent money home every month after I enlisted and kept sending it up until the day she died suddenly of an aneurysm."

"I'm so sorry about your mother's passing," Nora

said, shaking her head. "Wow. As an enlisted man, how did you make enough to send some home?"

"I ate in the chow hall and lived on post. I didn't party or spend money on civilian clothes or booze. Mom needed it. I gave it to her."

"You were a good son to her," Nora said.

His chest tightened. "She died of an aneurysm a couple of weeks before she was due to move to Texas where I'd purchased a house for her."

"Wow. And, let me guess, you blame yourself for not getting her to Texas sooner...?" Her gaze captured his.

Her words hit home, and he winced. "Yeah. I should've done it sooner."

"Can't bring people back with regrets." Nora stared into her coffee cup. "I learned that. The only thing I could do was move forward and get on with living. I wanted to get away from Milwaukee and the home I'd shared with my mother. Not knowing where else to go, I wandered past a realtor's office and stepped into a recruiter's office. I had my nursing degree, they wanted and needed nurses on active duty. I signed up, they put me through some officer training and here I am." She held her arms out.

"Playing volleyball in Afghanistan, working on your tan during the day and helping soldiers at night." Rucker gave her a brief smile. "I, for one, appreciate what you're doing for our guys and gals."

"I do the best I can," she said softly. "I just wish I

could do more. I'd rather stay here than redeploy back to the States, but they're afraid if they keep us here too long, we'll burn out or get PTSD."

"One week, huh?"

She nodded. "One week."

"In my field, one week to redeploy back to the States is a dangerous time. Anything can happen and usually does."

"Yeah, but you guys are on the frontlines, if not behind enemy lines. I'm back here. What could happen?"

Rucker flinched. "Oh, sweetheart, you didn't just say that..." He glanced around, hoping no one heard her tempt fate with those dreaded words *What could happen?*

Nora grinned. "You're not superstitious, are you?"

"In what we do, we can't afford not to be," he said, tossing salt over his shoulder.

"I'll be fine," she said in a reassuring, nurse's voice.

"Stop," he said, holding up his hand. "You're only digging the hole deeper." He tossed more salt over his other shoulder.

Nora laughed.

"Don't laugh." He handed her the saltshaker. "Do it."

"I'm not tossing salt over my shoulder. Someone has to clean the mess hall."

Rucker leaned close and shook salt over her shoulder. "I don't know if it counts if someone else throws salt over your shoulder, but I figure you now need every bit of luck you can get."

"You're a fighter but afraid of a little bad luck." Nora shook her head. "Those two things don't seem to go together."

"You'd be surprised how easily my guys are freaked by the littlest things."

"And you," she reminded him.

"You asking *what could happen?* isn't a little thing. That's in-your-face tempting fate." Rucker was laying it on thick to keep her grinning, but deep down, he believed what he was saying. And it didn't make a difference the amount of education he had or the statistics that predicted outcomes. His gut told him she'd just tempted fate with her statement. Maybe he was overthinking things. Now, he was worried she wouldn't make it back to the States alive.

NORA LIKED RUCKER. He was the first guy who'd walked away without an argument since she'd arrived at the base in Afghanistan. He'd meant what he'd said and proved it. His dark brown hair and deep green eyes, coupled with broad shoulders and a narrow waist, made him even more attractive. Not all the men were in as good a shape as Rucker. And he seemed to have a very determined attitude.

She hadn't known what to expect when she'd

deployed. Being the center of attention of almost every single male on the base hadn't been one of her expectations. She'd only ever considered herself average in the looks department. But when the men outnumbered women by more than ten to one, she guessed average appearance moved up in the ranks.

"Where did you learn to play volleyball?" Rucker asked, changing the subject of her leaving and her flippant comment about what could happen in one week.

"I was on the volleyball team in high school. It got me a scholarship to a small university in my home state of Minnesota, where I got my Bachelor of Science degree in Nursing."

"It takes someone special to be a nurse," he stated. "Is that what you always wanted to be?"

She shook her head. "I wanted to be a firefighter when I was in high school."

"What made you change your mind?"

She stared down at the coffee growing cold in her mug. "My mother was diagnosed with cancer when I was a senior in high school. I wanted to help but felt like I didn't know enough to be of assistance." She looked up. "She made it through chemo and radiation treatments and still came to all of my volleyball games. I thought she was in the clear."

"She wasn't?" Rucker asked, his tone low and gentle.

"She didn't tell me any different. When I got the

scholarship, I told her I wanted to stay close to home to be with her. She insisted I go and play volleyball for the university. I was pretty good and played for the first two years I was there. I quit the team in my third year to start the nursing program. I didn't know there was anything wrong back home. I called every week to talk to Mom. She never let on that she was sick." She forced a smile. "But you don't want my sob story. You probably want to know what's going on around here."

He set his mug on the table. "If we were alone in a coffee bar back in the States, I'd reach across the table and take your hand."

"Oh, please. Don't do that." She looked around the mess hall, half expecting someone might have overheard Rucker's comment. "You're enlisted. I'm an officer. That would get us into a whole lot of trouble."

"Yeah, but we're also two human beings. I wouldn't be human if I didn't feel empathy for you and want to provide comfort."

She set her coffee cup on the table and laid her hands in her lap. "I'll be satisfied with the thought. Thank you."

"Doesn't seem like enough. When did you find out your mother was sick?"

She swallowed the sadness that welled in her throat every time she remembered coming home to find out her mother had been keeping her illness from her. "It wasn't until I went home for Christmas in my senior year that I realized she'd been lying to me for a while." She laughed in lieu of sobbing. "I don't care who they are, old people don't always tell the truth."

"How long had she been keeping her sickness from you?"

"She'd known the cancer had returned halfway through my junior year. I hadn't gone home that summer because I'd been working hard to get my coursework and clinical hours in the nursing program. When I went home at Christmas…" Nora gulped. "She wasn't the same person. She'd lost so much weight and looked twenty years older."

"Did you stay home that last semester?" Rucker asked.

"Mom insisted I go back to school and finish what I'd started. Like your mother, she hadn't gone to college. She wanted her only child to graduate. She was afraid that if I stayed home to take care of her, I wouldn't finish my nursing degree."

"I heard from a buddy of mine that those programs can be hard to get into," he said. "I can see why she wouldn't want you to drop everything in your life to take care of her."

Nora gave him a watery smile. "That's what she said. As soon as my last final was over, I returned to my hometown. I became her nurse. She lasted another three months before she slipped away."

"That's when you joined the Army?"

She shook her head. "Dad was so heartbroken, I stayed a few months until he was feeling better. I got a job at a local emergency room. On weekends, my father and I worked on cleaning out the house and getting it ready to put on the market."

"Is your dad still alive?" Rucker asked.

Nora nodded. "He lives in Texas. He moved to a small house with a big backyard." She forced a smile. "He has a garden, and all the ladies in his retirement community think he's the cat's meow. He still misses Mom, but he's getting on with his life."

Rucker tilted his head. "When did you join the military?"

"When Dad sold the house and moved into his retirement community. I worried about him, but he's doing better."

"And you?"

"I miss her. But she'd whip my ass if I wallowed in self-pity for more than a moment. She was a strong woman and expected me to be the same."

Rucker grinned. "From what I've seen, you are."

Nora gave him a skeptical look. "You've only seen me playing volleyball. It's just a game." Not that she'd admit it, but she was a real softy when it came to caring for the sick and injured.

"If you're half as good at nursing, which I'm willing to bet you are, you're amazing." He started to reach across the table for her hand. Before he actually touched her, he grabbed the saltshaker and shook it over his cold breakfast.

"You just got in this morning?" Nora asked.

Rucker nodded.

"How long will you be here?" she asked.

"I don't know."

"What do you mean, you don't know? I thought when people were deployed, they were given a specific timeframe."

"Most people are. We're deployed where and when needed."

Nora frowned. "What are you? Some kind of special forces team?"

His lips pressed together. "Can't say."

She sat back. He was some kind of Special Forces. "Army, right?"

He nodded.

That would make him Delta Force. The elite of the elite. A very skilled soldier who undertook incredibly dangerous missions. She gulped and stopped herself from reaching across the table to take his hand. "Well, I hope all goes well while you and your team are here."

"Thanks."

A man hurried across the chow hall wearing shorts and an Army T-shirt. He headed directly toward their table.

Nora didn't recognize him. "Expecting someone?" she asked Rucker, tipping her head toward the man.

Rucker turned, a frown pulling his eyebrows together. "Why the hell's Dash awake?"

Nora frowned. "Dash? Please tell me that's his callsign, not his real name."

Rucker laughed. "It should be his real name. He's first into the fight, and he's fast." Rucker stood and faced his teammate. "What's up?"

"CO wants us all in the Tactical Operations Center," Dash said. "On the double."

"Guess that's my cue to exit." Rucker turned to Nora. "I enjoyed our talk."

She nodded. "Me, too."

Dash grinned. "Tell you what…I'll stay and finish your conversation while you see what the commander wants."

Rucker hooked Dash's arm twisted it up behind his back, and gave him a shove toward the door. "You heard the CO, he wants all of us." Rucker winked at Nora. "I hope to see you on the volleyball court before you leave."

"Same. Good luck." Nora's gaze followed Rucker's broad shoulders and tight ass out of the chow hall. Too bad she'd only be there another week before she shipped out. She would've enjoyed more volleyball and coffee with the Delta Force operative.

He'd probably be on maneuvers that entire week.

She stacked her tray and coffee cup in the collection area and left the chow hall, heading for the building where she shared her quarters with Beth

Drennan, a nurse she'd become friends with during their deployment together.

As close as they were, Nora didn't bring up her conversation with the Delta. With only a week left at the base, she probably wouldn't run into him again. Though she would like to see him again, she prayed he didn't end up in the hospital.

ABOUT THE AUTHOR

ELLE JAMES also writing as MYLA JACKSON is a *New York Times* and *USA Today* Bestselling author of books including cowboys, intrigues and paranormal adventures that keep her readers on the edges of their seats. When she's not at her computer, she's traveling, snow skiing, boating, or riding her ATV, dreaming up new stories. Learn more about Elle James at www.ellejames.com

Website | Facebook | Twitter | GoodReads | Newsletter | BookBub | Amazon

Or visit her alter ego Myla Jackson at mylajackson.com
Website | Facebook | Twitter | Newsletter

Follow Me!
www.ellejames.com
ellejamesauthor@gmail.com

ALSO BY ELLE JAMES

Iron Horse Legacy

Soldier's Duty (#1)

Ranger's Baby (#2)

Marine's Promise (#3)

SEAL's Vow (#4)

Warrior's Resolve (#5)

Drake (#6)

Grimm (#7)

Murdock (#8)

Utah (#9)

Judge (#10)

Bayou Brotherhood Protectors

Remy (#1)

Brotherhood Protectors Yellowstone

Saving Kyla (#1)

Saving Chelsea (#2)

Saving Amanda (#3)

Saving Liliana (#4)

Saving Breely (#5)

Saving Savvie (#6)

Saving Jenna (#7)

Brotherhood Protectors Colorado

SEAL Salvation (#1)

Rocky Mountain Rescue (#2)

Ranger Redemption (#3)

Tactical Takeover (#4)

Colorado Conspiracy (#5)

Rocky Mountain Madness (#6)

Free Fall (#7)

Colorado Cold Case (#8)

Fool's Folly (#9)

Colorado Free Rein (#10)

Rocky Mountain Venom (#11)

Brotherhood Protectors

Montana SEAL (#1)

Bride Protector SEAL (#2)

Montana D-Force (#3)

Cowboy D-Force (#4)

Montana Ranger (#5)

Montana Dog Soldier (#6)

Montana SEAL Daddy (#7)

Montana Ranger's Wedding Vow (#8)

Montana SEAL Undercover Daddy (#9)

Cape Cod SEAL Rescue (#10)

Montana SEAL Friendly Fire (#11)

Montana SEAL's Mail-Order Bride (#12)

SEAL Justice (#13)

Ranger Creed (#14)

Delta Force Rescue (#15)

Dog Days of Christmas (#16)

Montana Rescue (#17)

Montana Ranger Returns (#18)

Hot SEAL Salty Dog (SEALs in Paradise)

Hot SEAL, Hawaiian Nights (SEALs in Paradise)

Hot SEAL Bachelor Party (SEALs in Paradise)

Hot SEAL, Independence Day (SEALs in Paradise)

Brotherhood Protectors Boxed Set 1

Brotherhood Protectors Boxed Set 2

Brotherhood Protectors Boxed Set 3

Brotherhood Protectors Boxed Set 4

Brotherhood Protectors Boxed Set 5

Brotherhood Protectors Boxed Set 6

Shadow Assassin

Delta Force Strong

Ivy's Delta (Delta Force 3 Crossover)

Breaking Silence (#1)

Breaking Rules (#2)

Breaking Away (#3)

Breaking Free (#4)

Breaking Hearts (#5)

Breaking Ties (#6)

Breaking Point (#7)

Breaking Dawn (#8)

Breaking Promises (#9)

Hearts & Heroes Series

Wyatt's War (#1)

Mack's Witness (#2)

Ronin's Return (#3)

Sam's Surrender (#4)

Hellfire Series

Hellfire, Texas (#1)

Justice Burning (#2)

Smoldering Desire (#3)

Hellfire in High Heels (#4)

Playing With Fire (#5)

Up in Flames (#6)

Total Meltdown (#7)

Take No Prisoners Series

SEAL's Honor (#1)

SEAL'S Desire (#2)

SEAL's Embrace (#3)

SEAL's Obsession (#4)

SEAL's Proposal (#5)

SEAL's Seduction (#6)

SEAL'S Defiance (#7)

SEAL's Deception (#8)

SEAL's Deliverance (#9)

SEAL's Ultimate Challenge (#10)

Texas Billionaire Club

Tarzan & Janine (#1)

Something To Talk About (#2)

Who's Your Daddy (#3)

Love & War (#4)

Billionaire Online Dating Service

The Billionaire Husband Test (#1)

The Billionaire Cinderella Test (#2)

The Billionaire Bride Test (#3)

The Billionaire Daddy Test (#4)

The Billionaire Matchmaker Test (#5)

The Billionaire Glitch Date (#6)

The Billionaire Perfect Date (#7) coming soon

The Billionaire Replacement Date (#8) coming soon

The Billionaire Wedding Date (#9) coming soon

Cajun Magic Mystery Series

Voodoo on the Bayou (#1)

Voodoo for Two (#2)

Deja Voodoo (#3)

Cajun Magic Mysteries Books 1-3

The Outriders

Homicide at Whiskey Gulch (#1)

Hideout at Whiskey Gulch (#2)

Held Hostage at Whiskey Gulch (#3)

Setup at Whiskey Gulch (#4)

Missing Witness at Whiskey Gulch (#5)

Cowboy Justice at Whiskey Gulch (#6)

Ballistic Cowboy

Hot Combat (#1)

Hot Target (#2)

Hot Zone (#3)

Hot Velocity (#4)

Declan's Defenders

Marine Force Recon (#1)

Show of Force (#2)

Full Force (#3)
Driving Force (#4)
Tactical Force (#5)
Disruptive Force (#6)

Mission: Six

One Intrepid SEAL
Two Dauntless Hearts
Three Courageous Words
Four Relentless Days
Five Ways to Surrender
Six Minutes to Midnight

SEAL Of My Own

Navy SEAL Survival
Navy SEAL Captive
Navy SEAL To Die For
Navy SEAL Six Pack

Devil's Shroud Series

Deadly Reckoning (#1)
Deadly Engagement (#2)
Deadly Liaisons (#3)
Deadly Allure (#4)
Deadly Obsession (#5)
Deadly Fall (#6)

Covert Cowboys Inc Series

Triggered (#1)

Taking Aim (#2)

Bodyguard Under Fire (#3)

Cowboy Resurrected (#4)

Navy SEAL Justice (#5)

Navy SEAL Newlywed (#6)

High Country Hideout (#7)

Clandestine Christmas (#8)

Thunder Horse Series

Hostage to Thunder Horse (#1)

Thunder Horse Heritage (#2)

Thunder Horse Redemption (#3)

Christmas at Thunder Horse Ranch (#4)

Demon Series

Hot Demon Nights (#1)

Demon's Embrace (#2)

Tempting the Demon (#3)

Lords of the Underworld

Witch's Initiation (#1)

Witch's Seduction (#2)

The Witch's Desire (#3)

Possessing the Witch (#4)

Stealth Operations Specialists (SOS)

Nick of Time

Alaskan Fantasy

Boys Behaving Badly Anthologies

Rogues (#1)

Blue Collar (#2)

Pirates (#3)

Stranded (#4)

First Responder (#5)

Silver Soldier's (#6)

Blown Away

Warrior's Conquest

Enslaved by the Viking Short Story

Conquests

Smokin' Hot Firemen

Protecting the Colton Bride

Protecting the Colton Bride & Colton's Cowboy Code

Heir to Murder

Secret Service Rescue

High Octane Heroes

Haunted

Engaged with the Boss

Cowboy Brigade

Time Raiders: The Whisper

Bundle of Trouble

Killer Body

Operation XOXO

An Unexpected Clue

Baby Bling

Under Suspicion, With Child

Texas-Size Secrets

Cowboy Sanctuary

Lakota Baby

Dakota Meltdown

Beneath the Texas Moon

Made in the USA
Columbia, SC
15 June 2025